LOCKET OF EMOTIONS

Locket of Emotions

LOCKET OF EMOTIONS

Locket of Emotions

Locket of Emotions

By Bella Ivy

Any references to historical events, real people, or real places are used fictitiously. Names, characters, and places are products of the author's imagination.

Cover Design by Cat Cover Design

Table of Contents

Locket of Emotions

Chapter One
The Locket

"Laura," her mother whispered weakly from the bed. "Come here."

Five-year-old Laura Paige looked up at her dad, who nodded. She carefully let go of her dad's arm and made her way over to the hospital bed where her mother was lying.

Monitors were beeping, and liquid pushed in and out of the tubes that surrounded her. The room was cold and empty, and the darkness outside only made it worse. Laura shivered as she approached her mother, who was looking so weak, so frail.

Laura thought if she hugged her mom, she might break her into little pieces, like the vase that she had accidentally shattered a few months ago.

She stood next to her mom, gently grabbing hold of her hand, and looked at her sadly.

"Mom?" Laura asked.

"My little Laura, my darling little Laura," Laura's mom whispered. "I know everything might seem scary right now, but don't you worry, okay?"

Laura nodded.

"You're a brave and beautiful girl, full of happiness and love. You will live a life of great wonders, changing the lives of those who meet you," her mom said.

She reached around her neck, pulled off a silver locket, and handed it to Laura. Closing her little fist around the locket, Laura's mother smiled.

"Will you take care of this for me?" she asked. "It's a very special locket. Full of unusual secrets and mysteries."

"I will, Mom," Laura said, tears dripping down her cheeks.

"Promise me you won't lose it?"

"I promise!" Laura said, her eyes twinkling as she held on tightly to the locket.

"That's my girl," her mom said with a smile. "Bring out the light in everyone, okay?"

Laura nodded, unsure of what her mother meant. She took the locket and hung it around her neck, letting it settle onto her dress. Laura looked up and smiled, but it faded away when she saw her mother again.

"Mommy?" she asked.

Her mother's eyes fluttered open. "Just resting, Laura. Mommy is just resting."

"I love you, Mom."

Her mother smiled again and put her hand over Laura's heart. "I'll always be right here, Laura. Whenever you think of me, know that I'm always with you."

Laura nodded again. "Can you tell me about our house in the clouds again?" she asked, her blue eyes shining.

Her mom and dad laughed. They sat together, and once again, Laura's mother told the story about their big house in the clouds, where no one is hurt or sad, and everyone loves each other, no matter what.

She described their house, how they'll live with hundreds of adorable pets and will have plenty of friends. Laura listened to her mom talk, imagining the house as her eyes closed.

Five hours later, Laura's mother passed away. Laura and her dad left the hospital, holding each other's hands, hearts heavy and full of grief. As they climbed into the car, Laura looked over at her dad.

"We'll see mommy again, right?"

"Of course, sweetie," Laura's dad said, blinking back tears. "We'll all be together at the house in the clouds someday."

Laura smiled. "I like that. Maybe that's why Mom said we'll see her later."

She nestled down into her car seat and leaned back. She played with her mother's locket the entire way home, thinking about her, wondering if she was having a grand adventure on her way to the house in the clouds.

When they finally arrived home, Laura picked up her box of crayons and started to draw in a notebook her mom gave her for her birthday last year. She drew them all in the hospital together, and then, she drew her mother picking up a few bags and flying to the home in the clouds. She also drew their old cat and dog in the sky, holding hands.

From the other room, she could hear her dad crying. Laura frowned and stood up, walking over to her dad's bedroom. She climbed up onto the bed and snuggled up next to him.

"Don't worry, Daddy," she said, patting his shoulder. "I'm still here." Laura smiled and pointed at his heart. "And Mommy said she will always be right here too."

Laura's dad wiped away his tears and smiled. He sighed and patted her on the head.

"You're right," he whispered. "I'll remember that."

He hugged her tightly, and for a moment, Laura felt all the sadness leave his mind. She liked the feeling so much, she decided to make him feel better every day, until his sadness was gone for good.

***

Ten years later, Laura knew her dad was happy once again, although there was still a little piece of sadness that would always remain. It bugged her that it never went away, but the more Laura learned and grew, the more she realized she would always have that piece of sadness too.

They both just missed her mom too much to carry on life exactly the same as before. But that little piece of sadness never stopped them from having fun together, like going to the movies, going on road trips, and spending everyday together, unless her dad was at work, or she was at school.

Laura also made many new friends, spending time with them whenever she wasn't with her dad. She had found her little corner of happiness.

Her dad also found a new source of happiness. A new woman, Cassandra, came into his life as well as Laura's, and soon, they were spending more and more time together. She adored Laura, seeing her as the daughter she never had, and Laura liked her well enough.

The woman also had a son, just a year older than Laura. His name was Ryan. The first time they met, Laura found herself mesmerized by him, wondering about all the sadness and fear and darkness inside him.

She thought she could change him too, just like she changed her dad's sadness, but the more they hung out, the more Laura realized she didn't like hanging out with Ryan that much. He had a mental barrier, something that wouldn't let her into his life.

One night, while Cassandra and her dad went out to dinner, Laura and Ryan watched a movie together. Laura looked over at him.

"This is an interesting movie, right?" she asked.

It was a classic superhero movie, and she had paused it for more popcorn.

"It's alright," Ryan said. "I wish we could see the hero lose for once. They *always* win. It's so predictable."

"Why?" Laura asked. "Shouldn't good always win?"

Ryan shrugged. "It's a nice change," he said, popping some of the fresh popcorn into his mouth.

Laura looked at him suspiciously. He shrugged and turned back to the movie, hitting play. As they watched the movie together, Laura figured she should try to keep a closer eye on Ryan, hoping to find a better way into his heart.

Chapter Two
Empath Discovered

One year later, Laura's dad and Cassandra got married. Cassandra became Laura's stepmom, and Ryan became her stepbrother. As much as she was overjoyed to have a new family, Laura still couldn't shake the feeling that something was terribly wrong with her new brother.

Still, she continued to shrug it off, unsure of why her head was bothering her so much. She didn't have time to stress about things she could not change. The four of them eventually moved into a new house together in a brand-new city, far from her childhood home, although her dad promised they'd go back and visit whenever they could.

On the morning of her first day of school, Laura stretched and looked at herself in the mirror. Yawning, she pulled out her makeup kit and put on the basics. She didn't want to go too crazy on the powders and creams just yet.

Besides, most of her stuff were still packed away in boxes. They had moved into the new house only a few weeks before, so much of their home was still a mess.

Laura smiled at herself in the mirror, tugging her loose blonde curls back into a ponytail.

"You got this," she whispered to herself. "New school, new faces, new teachers."

Laura sighed and reached for her mother's locket. Putting it on, Laura looked at her reflection one more time and smiled. Now, her mom would be with her on her first day of school too.

Knocking echoed on the bathroom door.

"Are you almost done yet? I gotta go!" Ryan whined on the other side.

Laura rolled her eyes at the impatience. "Just a few more minutes," Laura said. "I'll be out soon!"

"You better be!" Ryan shouted. He stomped away from the bathroom door and down the hall.

Not wanting to feel more of her brother's wrath, Laura quickly finished up her morning routine and ran downstairs to the kitchen while Ryan slipped into the bathroom behind her.

She took a seat at the counter, pulling a few pancakes off the center plate. Her dad was happily making more, whistling a tune as he scrambled the eggs.

"Good morning, sunshine!" he said, bringing the pan over.

"Good morning, Dad," Laura answered with a smile.

Her dad was in a happy mood. She wondered if it was because of the job interview he had later today.

"How's my little girl doing this morning?"

Laura laughed. "I'm not that little anymore, Dad," she said.

"I know, I know," he said with a fake sniff. "I just hope you like your new school.

Cassandra says it's the best in the city." He grinned. "Anything for the best two kids a dad could have!" Her dad spun around and went back to the stove, scrambling a few more eggs.

Ryan came down ten minutes later. Together, they finished their breakfasts, grabbed their bags, and walked out the door. Laura learned the way to the bus stop like it was the back of her hand, and even made sure they got the student passes for the city buses.

They turned the corner and made their way down the shaded street, where a few people were already up and walking their dogs on the cool September morning. Laura looked up at the trees, spotting leaves on a few of them already turning colors.

Summer was finally over, and school was starting once again. She smiled.

They stopped at the bus stop five minutes ahead of schedule. While they waited, Laura fidgeted with her mom's locket, looking at the shiny silver on the outside.

"Have you ever opened it?" Ryan asked.

"No," Laura said.

"Why not?"

Laura shrugged. "Not sure."

She had always wondered what was inside, but she never found the right time to open it. Laura had always assumed it was a picture of her mom, or even them all together as a family. Whatever was inside, Laura was just fine keeping it a secret.

Ryan laughed. "Why don't we just open it up right now then?"

Laura took a step back. "No!" She sighed and shook her head. "No, I don't want to."

"Then I'll do it." Ryan reached forward and broke the chain off her neck. He laughed. "Man, that's a cheap piece of jewelry!"

"Give it back!" Laura shouted, reaching for her locket.

Ryan held it high above his head and laughed again. "It's just a locket, Laura, calm down!"

He pushed the button on the clasp, and the locket swung open. Laura gasped as a rainbow of colors poured out like a never-ending waterfall.

"Huh," Ryan said. "It's just a picture."

But Laura wasn't paying attention. She was still watching the colors that came out of the locket. The colors swirled around, and she reached up, snatching the locket out of his hand.

Laura turned to her brother. She blinked and rubbed her eyes. Ryan was a mixture of intense red and blue colors. She blinked again, and this time, she felt a wave of sadness and anger crash onto her. Laura stumbled backwards, reaching for the stop sign next to her.

"What's gotten into you?" Ryan asked.

Laura shook her head and breathed heavily. She closed the locket, and suddenly, all the intense emotions went away. She had never felt that sad or that angry before. That had to be someone else's feelings. But the only one around was Ryan.

"Sorry," she whispered. "Felt dizzy for a second."

"Whatever, weirdo," Ryan said. He looked up. "Look, the bus is here."

She looked up and nodded. They climbed onto the bus, showing their passes to the driver. They sat near the back doors while waiting for several other people to board.

A few teens who were Laura's age climbed on with backpacks too, and they laughed while deep in conversation.

The entire bus ride to the inner city, Laura studied her locket. She realized she had never actually looked at it close enough. She would only drape it around her neck and leave it be. The outside of the locket had five gems, each one a different color: yellow, red, blue, green, and purple.

Laura traced the gems, wondering what they were. They were so beautiful and glistened under the sun rays shining through the window. She wondered if they had anything to do with the colors that poured out of the locket.

As the bus drove through the city, picking up several more passengers along the way, Laura closed her eyes, trying to block out all the noise in her head that still lingered from when Ryan opened the locket.

She could feel all sorts of new emotions surrounding her, ones that weren't her own. She felt sadness, but it was a minor sadness that wasn't as overwhelming as the one that sat next to her, deep within her stepbrother's mind. Laura shook her head.

"No, it can't be. I must not have gotten enough sleep," Laura whispered to herself.

"Yeah, you're telling me. I could hear you rolling around in bed all the way from my room," Ryan teased upon hearing her.

When they arrived at the school, Laura jumped off the bus and ran inside. She hadn't been there before, since this was an entirely new city for her, and decided to walk to the office to ask for a map. As she walked, Laura paused, noticing a quiet courtyard with a tree growing in the middle of the field.

Grass and flowers were all around, and she smiled. It was nice and quiet. She derailed and headed towards the courtyard instead of the office and took a seat under the tree. It was just too beautiful to not admire, even if for just a minute.

Opening up her locket again, the colors swirled, this time, into a small rainbow image, forming the face of her mom, smiling, "So, I see you finally opened up the locket," she said.

"Mom? Is that really you?" Laura whispered.

"I'm sure you may have a lot of questions," her mother said. "I'll start with one: this is a recording." She smiled, looking Laura in the eyes. "You and I come from a long line of empaths, Laura. You'll learn how to control your emotions, learn how to read others' emotions and, with enough practice, learn how to control them."

"How? I don't understand," Laura whispered.

"Laura, I left you a chest. Your father knows where it is. Use this locket to unlock it, and there, your training will begin," her mother continued. "And remember, always use this gift for good." Her mom turned her head. "I can sense that your mind feels a little overwhelmed from when you first opened the locket. I can take your powers away until you're ready to open the locket again."

Laura nodded. She closed her eyes, and suddenly, the noise in her head stopped. She closed her locket, a few drops of tears dripping from her eyes as she remembered her mom, took a deep breath, and looked around.

The little garden in the school was still quiet and peaceful, and a few birds chirped on the branches above.

"Oh!" a voice said behind her.

Laura jumped and turned around. A boy with sandy blonde hair and hazel eyes stood near the gates of the courtyard.

"Sorry," he said. "I didn't mean to scare you."

"That's okay," Laura said. She smiled.

"You must be new here," he said. He held out his hand. "I'm Lucas."

Laura reached up, took his hand, and introduced herself. "Laura," she said. "Just starting today!"

"What grade are you in?" Lucas asked, his hazel eyes twinkling in the morning sunlight.

"I'm a junior," she replied.

"Hey, me too!" Lucas laughed. His laugh was one of the most wonderful sounds Laura had ever heard, and she couldn't help but smile as his affectionate laugh. "I'll show you around the school. Lucky for you, Laura, I'm the best tour guide you could ever ask for."

"Oh, really? I guess I'll be the judge of that." Laura smiled again.

"Sure am! You can count on me!" Lucas grinned. "We should get your schedule first."

Laura laughed and finally broke eye contact. She looked down at the grass, still smiling. "You're right. I almost forgot. First day jitters, I guess."

She followed him out of the garden and into the office just across the way. Lucas guided her to the main part of the building, where they gave her a locker number, a student handbook, a few other important papers, and finally, her class schedule and a map.

Lucas took her schedule and looked it over.

"Hey," he said, pointing at their last two classes. "We have Ceramics and English Lit together!"

"We do?" Laura asked excitedly.

She looked down at her schedule. Everything seemed normal, just like her school back in her hometown.

"And lunch together!" Lucas exclaimed. "I'll introduce you to some of my friends later." He looked at his watch. "Come on, let's get that tour out of the way before first period."

Together, they walked through the school. At first, Laura was only half listening, still focused on her locket, wondering what other things her mom had waiting for her at home.

She was constantly going over the word "empath" in her head until Lucas stopped walking. She bumped into him and laughed. Lucas laughed too.

"There are quiet little gardens all over campus," he said, showing her another one. "In case you ever need a break from all the craziness inside."

"Really? That's so awesome. I love gardens!" Laura cheered, her eyes wide.

"Right?" Lucas grinned. "They're great for study groups too."

They continued the tour. Lucas showed her where the best place to sit for lunch was, as well as all the shortcuts and tips for each building. They were all separated by subject area, each with tons of classrooms, one for each grade.

The middle of the school was where all the high school students hung out, the *Hub*, as many of them called it. All their lockers were there, along with tables, couches, and a small common area.

"This is the coolest high school I've ever been to," Laura said.

"Yeah, it used to be a mall, but then the mall moved to a different town after it was bought out, and the high school took over," Lucas explained. "They made it so much better, in my opinion."

"So, the Hub is basically where you get all the student information," Lucas explained. "You can hang out there between classes also. There's usually all kinds of snacks and refreshments, free of charge." He looked down at the locker number the office secretary had written down for Laura. "Hey, look at that!"

"What is it? Look at what?" Laura asked.

"You're just a few lockers down from me!" He led the way, stopping at a row of lockers in the Hub, and grinned, pointing at the one in front of him.

Laura looked at her number and back at the locker. She laughed and entered the combination. All of her textbooks and a few school supplies were already inside, including a letter that said "Welcome!" on it. Laura smiled. Maybe going to a school in the city wouldn't be too bad after all.

As she loaded some of her books from the locker into her bag, Laura noticed that Ryan was already hanging around a crowd of boys. They pushed through the Hub, laughing loudly and mocking the younger students.

"Ugh," Lucas said. "Don't worry about them."

"Why?" Laura asked.

"They're just here to hang out, not to learn or anything." Lucas sighed. "They like to bully newcomers and the freshmen."

Laura narrowed her eyes at Ryan, who seemed right at home with them. "Sure seems like it."

A bell soon chimed throughout the school hallways, and students started to zip up their bags, gather their belongings, and walk out of the Hub. Everyone walked to their classrooms, and Lucas smiled at Laura.

"I'll see you around!" he shouted, giving her a small salute, before taking off into the crowd of students.

Laura nodded and started to walk to her first class, Calculus. She followed the crowd, getting lost in thought as she walked down the halls. Her locket and her mother were both still strongly ingrained in her mind, and she couldn't wait to go home and see what was waiting for her in the chest.

She bumped into Ryan while walking through the door to her classroom.

"Watch where you're goi--" he paused, seeing that it was Laura. "Oh, it's you," he mumbled. "Way to ditch me back there."

"Seems like you made some new friends already," Laura said, looking at the group nearby.

Ryan nodded. "They're alright. Where'd you run off to anyway?"

"To find the nurse," Laura lied. "My head was killing me, and she gave me some painkillers to help me out."

Shrugging, Ryan moved away from the door. "See you after school," he said, waving his hand. "I'll leave without you if you're not at the bus stop by 3pm sharp."

Laura rolled her eyes and continued walking. A few students were already there, joking and shoving each other around. She settled down in the row closest to the window, not too far from the front nor from the back.

It was perfectly in the middle, and she could look out the window and stare at the beautiful garden whenever she needed to. For the rest of the day, Laura was content with school life. With each class that passed by, the locket moved further to the back of her mind.

A girl with braided black hair and red glasses happened to be in every class with her, and every now and then, she'd look at Laura, then turn back to her desk, paying attention to the teacher at the front.

Laura wondered if the girl was just too shy to come up and say hello, or if there was another reason why she couldn't stop staring. Shrugging it off, Laura decided that if this quiet girl was in her next class, she'd go right up to the girl and learn her name. Better to make more friends at a new school than to have none at all.

By her fourth class, Laura marched up to the girl and held out her hand.

"Hi," she said. "I'm Laura. Want to sit with me?"

The girl, slightly taken aback, shook her hand. "I'm Shelby. I'd love to sit with you!"

She grinned. Shelby followed Laura and sat next to her in their History class.

Pulling out her schedule, Laura looked it over and showed it to Shelby. Shelby laughed and pulled out her own.

"How did we end up in all the same classes?" she asked.

"No idea!" Laura said. "Want to sit with me in all the others too?" She smiled. "I noticed that you kept looking at me during Chemistry. What was that all about?"

Shelby blushed. "Sorry," she apologized. "I-I don't have a lot of friends here. I saw that you're new, and I was just trying to pick up the courage to go and talk to you!" Shelby looked down at the ground. "I'm glad you came up and talked to me instead."

"I thought so," Laura said. "Don't worry, I'll be your friend."

After History, they walked into the cafeteria together for lunch. Shelby grinned.

"I typically like to eat my lunch at my favorite spot out in the courtyard. Do you want to join me?" she asked.

"I can't," Laura declined. "I promised Lucas I'd eat lunch with him and his friends."

Shelby froze. "Lucas Winter?" she asked quietly. "I can't go there," she muttered.

"I'm sure Lucas will be okay with it!" Laura said with a smile. "The more the merrier, right? Come on, let's go find them!"

The two teens crossed the cafeteria and ran outside into the nearest garden, where they found Lucas, another boy, and another girl. Lucas smiled and waved at Laura, gesturing her to join him. Laura turned to Shelby and nodded.

They both took a seat on the grass, and Lucas introduced Kyle and Tara, his best friends. Laura introduced them to Shelby, who shyly waved at the group. The five of them enjoyed lunch together, talking about their day so far and welcoming Laura to the school.

Kyle and Tara both had a million questions, and Laura answered them all as best as she could. They asked her about her old town and what it was like there, since none of them had ever been out of the city before.

"I've always loved that small town vibe," Tara said. "It seems so magical."

"It really is!" Laura exclaimed with a smile. "My mom and I would spend hours in our garden, planting flowers and just listening to the beautiful birds chirping, watching the world blossom around us." She sighed, reaching up to touch her locket. "Not a day passes by where I don't wish that she was still with us. Things just haven't been the same without her."

"What happened to her?" Kyle asked. Laura looked down at the grass. "She passed away when I was five," she explained, holding on tightly to her locket. "I miss her every day, even when I was really little." She wiped away her tears and looked up at her new friends. "Sorry," she said. "Didn't mean to get sappy there."

Shelby leaned over and hugged her. "I'm so sorry. I know the feeling. I lost my mom when I was really young too," she said quietly. "One of the best women in the world. Dad never wanted to replace her. He said there's no woman in the world who could ever compete, so it's just the two of us." She blushed and returned to her notebook, scribbling away inside it.

Lunch ended on that note, and soon, the five of them parted ways. The rest of the school day, Laura wondered about her locket again, getting lost in thought so much that Shelby would often poke her in the arm to bring her back to reality. Laura would jump and remember to continue to pay attention to the teacher.

Lucas helped her also in the last two classes, and the three of them sat next to each other, passing notes back and forth as the teachers went over some classroom rules. They giggled, and Laura learned a few new things about Shelby. By the end of the school day, Laura and Shelby had become best friends.

When the final bell rang, Lucas walked with Laura and Shelby to the bus stop.

"I live nearby," he said, writing down his phone number. "If you ever want to hang out after school." He grinned and waved goodbye.

Laura smiled and tucked his number away in her pocket. "Isn't he the best?" she asked Shelby.

Shelby nodded. "He is," she said. She laughed. "I used to have a crush on him, until I realized it was just a friend crush."

"Shut up," Laura said with a grin. "That is the cutest thing ever!"

Shelby laughed. "What do you think of him?"

Laura thought for a moment. She did think that Lucas was very handsome, but at the same time, she wasn't sure if she could ever make a move. After all, she had only met him today! Laura smiled at that thought and turned back to Shelby.

"So, you were on the bus with me this morning too?"

"Actually, I think we live in the same neighborhood," Shelby admitted. "Just a block away from each other." She smiled. "I was running late this morning though, so my dad dropped me off at school today." She giggled. "Imagine being late on your first day of school!"

"It could be worse!" Laura chuckled.

The bus pulled up. Ryan was nowhere to be seen, so Laura boarded the bus without him. She figured he was probably off with his new friends. The bus ride home was a lot shorter than it was in the morning, less stops for people to get on and off as it was only mid-afternoon.

During the journey, she connected more and more with Shelby, giggling and laughing at each other's jokes. When they finally said goodbye, Laura unlocked her front door, ran upstairs to her room, and collapsed on her bed. She fell asleep, ignoring the same question that had been bugging her all day.

Chapter Three
Waves of Emotions

Laura didn't get to rest for too long. The questions were too much, overwhelming her mind even as she tried to shut them off, and finally, she sat up and turned her locket around, opening it one more time. The colors poured out and surrounded her once again, and the noise started.

But this time, it was so much quieter than it had been at the bus stop this morning. Her mother didn't appear again, and the blue gemstone lit up on the locket lid. Laura gasped, suddenly realizing what the gemstones on the outside meant.

"They're emotions!" she whispered.

She jumped out of bed and ran down the stairs to the basement. Grabbing a flashlight, Laura looked around the dark basement, searching for the chest her mother was talking about. A lot of unpacked boxes were still down there, but she knew they had put the chest downstairs.

Laura spotted it on a shelf, extremely dusty, but still slightly uncovered. Pulling it off the shelf, she walked back upstairs, carrying the small chest in her hands.

No one else was home yet. Her stepmom was working until six that night, her dad wouldn't be back from his interview until after seven, and Ryan would only come home when it was time for dinner. She had the whole house to herself.

Smiling, Laura locked her bedroom door and set her mother's chest down on the floor. The lock was exactly the shape of the locket, just as her mom had mentioned earlier. Laura took off the locket and pressed it into the lock. The lid of the chest swung open.

Laura gasped as she looked inside. It was filled with little notebooks, gemstones, and a letter from her mother. Laura put her locket back on and opened up the letter first. She sat there, reading the words.

Dearest Laura,

If you're reading this, it means you've finally turned sixteen. My little girl is all grown up! It is finally time that you learn the truth, something very important that I've been keeping from you for years.

This locket and chest contain materials about your training. You see, you and I come from a long line of empaths. We are able to control the emotions of others. Of course, it's easy to turn them on and off, but at first, it can be very overwhelming, and you may feel like you're going crazy.

I've left you a set of instructions and videos to watch so you can learn how to control your powers.

I guess I should explain what those powers are. You see, your locket helps you see what people are feeling. It works like one of those toy mood rings you always loved to try on.

But with you, you can change the emotions of others. You can take away someone's sadness and turn it into happiness. You can take away anger and replace it with calmness. You get the rest.

There is a catch though. You can only change their emotions when you are touching them, and you can only change the emotion of one person at a time. For a moment, you may capture their emotion, and it will be overwhelming at first. But the more you learn to control it, the better you'll become at handling it.

Just practice and train. You'll become a fully-realized empath eventually. Always use this power for good, and don't let the darkness consume you as you do. Hang on tight to that locket, and remember, you are a light to this world. Be that light for others, like you have always been for me.

From our house in the clouds.

Lots of Love,

Mom

Laura sniffled, wiping a few tears away. She hugged the letter tightly, folded it up, and hid it inside her diary. No one would think to look in there, plus, she wanted to keep her mother's words close to her. She pulled the chest closer to her and started to look around inside.

There were a few notebooks with instructions. Each one was labeled like the notebooks she had in her classes, and Laura sorted through them, smiling at her mom's organization skills. She looked at the faded notebooks and decided to get them digitalized later.

Laura even found letters from her grandmother and her great-grandmother, each passed down from generation to generation.

"It really does run in the family," Laura whispered, looking at all the notes and heartfelt messages.

She sighed and looked at her new homework assignment. As she opened up the first notebook, her bedroom door swung open.

"What do you want for dinner?" Ryan asked, standing at the doorway. His eyes narrowed as he looked at all the notebooks and papers scattered in the room. "What's all that?" he asked.

"Nothing," Laura said, tossing them all back inside the chest. "You said something about dinner?"

Ryan stared at her for a minute longer, his eyes going down to the locket around her neck. His eyes raised for a moment, and he smiled.

"Mom wants to know what you want for dinner. She's coming home late. Picking stuff up on her way back."

Laura's heart was beating, but she wasn't sure why. "Oh, I'm not sure. Tell her anything's fine with me."

"Alright, suit yourself, but don't come complaining to me when you don't like it." Ryan pulled his phone out of his pocket and sent a text. "Saw you made some friends today," he said, looking up from his phone.

Laura nodded. "Yeah, I did." She smiled. "You did too, it looks like."

Ryan grinned. "They're pretty cool." He shrugged. "Not sure if I'll stick with them all year though, not really my style. I'm more of a solo type."

"Are you sure?" Laura questioned. "Everyone needs friends. It's how we get by in this world in one piece."

Her stepbrother shrugged again. "Whatever," he said.

He left her room and wandered down the hallway to his own bunker. As soon as he left, Laura let out a sigh of relief. The same sadness that she had felt this morning on the bus returned. It was heavy in her heart, and she wasn't exactly sure why.

But as she watched her brother leave, something clicked in her mind. Ryan couldn't be feeling sad, could he? She quietly got up and stood outside his room. Music blasted loudly from inside, and the sad emotion grew more intense. Laura took a few steps back and ran to her room. It was Ryan.

Laura sat down on her bed and pulled out the first guide. She spent the rest of the evening reading through it and taking notes, practicing a few of the moves on herself. Her mother and everyone else before her had been so thorough that it didn't take her long to get in the zone and figure out what to do.

Eventually, her stepmom came home with dinner, and she put all the information back into the chest. She locked it again and ran down to the dining room, smelling a delicious aroma of fried rice on the way down.

Her stepmom put the last box of Chinese food down on the table when Laura's dad walked in through the front door.

"Ah, it's good to see my beautiful family!" he cried out with a smile, giving Cassandra a kiss on the cheek. "I hope everyone had the best day ever!"

"You sound like you had a great day," Laura said with a smile.

She noticed all the yellow rays of magic that just seemed to bounce off of her dad. He was so giddy that it turned into a rainbow of colors at times.

"Well, my dear Laura, my sweet little angel," Laura's dad said, "you're looking at the newest professor of Economics at Wilmer University!"

"No way! That's totally awesome!" Laura beamed.

She jumped up and hugged her dad. Her stepmom grinned and hugged him too, while her stepbrother remained sitting at the table, carefully reaching for the food, hoping no one would see. However, his mom noticed and smacked his hand away for being rude, and everyone else took a seat.

As they ate, everyone at the table took a moment to share their graces and talk about their day. Laura was the most enthusiastic about her new school, while Ryan only offered a shrug and a few lackluster comments.

They devoured their dinner, and a few minutes later, Laura and Ryan cleaned up the boxes and paper plates while their parents retreated to the living room to relax and put their feet up after a long day. Laura looked at her stepbrother, noticing the dark blue and black squiggles that seemed to pour out of him. That must have been the sadness she felt earlier.

Curious, Laura purposefully dropped a plate onto the ground. Ryan groaned and reached forward, and she reached her hand at the same time. When their hands briefly touched, Laura practiced sending a wave of happiness to her stepbrother.

He drew his hand back sharply. "Hey! What are you doing?" he yelled, shooting daggers through his eyes at Laura.

"What are you talking about?" Laura asked.

"You just did something to me, to my hand," Ryan yelled. He glared at her.

Laura shrugged. "I must've shocked you," she lied, hoping he wouldn't catch on to her powers. "I'm sorry," she mumbled. "Didn't mean to. I was just trying to get the plate."

"Whatever, weirdo," Ryan said.

He stood up and grabbed the trash bag. Laura picked up the recycling and followed her stepbrother outside.

When they reached the trash bins, Laura looked at Ryan with curiosity again.

"Ryan, are you happy?" Laura asked as she threw the plastic bottles into the recycling bin.

"What's that supposed to mean?" Ryan asked.

"Sorry," Laura said again. "I was just curious. I meant like, are you happy with the new school and our new house?" She smiled nervously. "I know it can be a lot to handle such a big change."

Ryan glared at her again. "I'm content," he said, tossing the trash bag into the bin. "I hate that word. Happy. What does that even mean anyway?" He scoffed. "Seems like the world can do with a lot less happiness. Why can't people just be content, nothing more, nothing less?"

Laura shrugged. She fiddled with her locket again, unsure of what he meant. Ryan had always seemed a bit depressed and moody, but she never made it her business to learn why. She always believed that if he wanted to tell her, he would, even if it would take years and years.

She sighed and followed Ryan back into the house. He marched straight upstairs to his room, slamming the door behind him.

Laura watched him go, slightly flinching at the sound of the slam.

Her stepmom looked up from her magazine and sighed.

"I'm sorry, Laura," she apologized. "Ryan can be a bit anti-social. Sometimes, it's best to just leave him be until he's ready to open up."

"Yeah," Laura whispered.

"I've read somewhere that change is good for depression. That's part of the reason why we moved," Cassandra continued. "Who knows, maybe the city life will be good for him." She smiled, but then it quickly faded away. "Anyway, your dad and I are about to watch a movie. Want to join us?"

Laura sensed the nervousness coming from her stepmom. She could tell that Cassandra found Ryan's behavior difficult to handle sometimes also.

"I think I'll skip the movie tonight," she said. "I have some homework I need to do. First day of school and all that." She smiled and quickly slipped up the stairs.

She paused halfway, hearing Cassandra say to her dad, "Homework? On the first day of school?"

"It happens more often than you would think," her dad responded. "They'll be fine. Don't worry. They're both good kids."

Laura sighed and went into her room, quietly shutting the door behind her. She sank onto her bed, looking at the chest full of her mom's notes. Moving over to the window, Laura looked up at the night sky, searching for the stars, as the sun slowly sank below the horizon.

She whispered, "Mom, I wish you were still here. I still have so much to learn, and I don't know where to start. Sometimes, I just feel so lonely and empty without you," Laura sighed again, feeling a tear slip down her cheek. She wiped it away. "I'll figure this whole thing out. Don't worry."

***

The next morning as Laura and Ryan climbed onto the bus, Ryan paused. "Hang on," he said. "I forgot something at home."

"You're going to be late," Laura reminded him.

"No, I won't," Ryan said. "I'll just catch the next bus! I'll see you there."

He jumped off and waved, running back towards their street.

Frowning, Laura found an empty seat and sat down by herself. For a moment, she thought Ryan had discovered her powers and was suddenly eager to break into her special chest and learn more about it, discovering her secret.

Her heart beat wildly in her chest, hoping that her treasure chest was stashed away somewhere safe and that she remembered to cover it well.

She closed her eyes, remembering where she had tucked it, up high in the corner of her closet, and her letter was safely secured away in her diary, which was hidden from plain sight. She relaxed again. Even if Ryan did find out, he would need her locket to access anything, which was hanging safely around her neck. Laura chuckled. She was safe for now.

Laura simply pushed it off as her brother probably just needed some space. Especially after last night. Or maybe he just forgot his phone at home.

Ryan *was* acting a little more strange than usual, but she wondered if it was just all the changes that were happening around them. Her thoughts were soon interrupted when Shelby plopped down in the seat next to Laura. Her friend smiled halfheartedly, then turned to look out the window.

"Morning, Shelby. Are you okay?" Laura asked.

"Hey, Laura. Yeah," Shelby said. "Everything's okay."

Laura frowned and glanced at her friend, not believing what she had just said. Shelby didn't seem as bright and cheery as she was yesterday. Slowly, she reached over with her knee and tapped Laura by accident. A wave of sadness and fatigue crashed onto Laura. Shaking her head, Laura turned to her friend and touched her shoulder.

"Hey," Laura said. "Are you ready for your second day of school?"

"Sure," Shelby whispered. "It's just another long day, I guess."

The bus pulled away from the stop and rumbled down the city streets. Laura watched as many of the other students on the bus put on their headphones and turned up their music, something that had become a morning routine for most of them.

Laura sent a burst of happiness into her friend, taking away the sadness. She would have to ask Shelby about it later.

"What about our ceramics class?" Laura asked. "I can't wait to make some pots and sculptures!"

Shelby smiled. A real smile this time. "You're right!" she said. Turning to Laura, Shelby cheered. "I heard that each group is supposed to be making some big project. Maybe we can collaborate with Lucas later!"

Laura grinned. Her powers actually worked, and Shelby didn't seem to notice at all.

"That sounds like a lot of fun," she said. "What do you think we'll have to make?"

"No clue. But we should start coming up with some ideas!" Shelby said.

She seemed to be in a much better mood now. During the rest of the bus ride to school, Shelby and Laura eagerly talked to each other about what they looked forward to in their classes that day, and Shelby pulled out her sketchbook.

"I think I'm going to do a drawing a day," she said. "In any class! That'll be my goal for the year."

"That sounds exciting," Laura said. "Why?"

"Just to practice," Shelby replied. "Someday, I'll be the best illustrator this world has ever seen."

Laura smiled again. That was a good goal to have in life. As they stepped off the bus, Laura fidgeted with her locket. They walked toward the Hub, laughing as they realized their lockers were right next to each other. She continued to play with her locket, wondering what kind of goal she wanted to accomplish. Something just as cool as Shelby's.

The more she played with her locket, the more Laura started to realize that the world was spinning around again. Too many emotions from others were pouring in, and she started to lose focus.

When Laura opened her eyes again, she looked around, realizing that she was in the nurse's office. Lucas was sitting next to the bed. As Laura sat up, Lucas jumped to his feet.

"Oh my gosh," he said. "You're awake!"

"What happened?" Laura asked.

"I walked up to say hi to you and Shelby," Lucas explained. "But you collapsed before I could say anything. Caught you just in time before you hit your head on the ground."

Laura reached up and touched her head. Everything felt calm now, and she sighed with relief. Her powers were acting up again, and they were getting worse the longer she was in the high school, surrounded by different people with all types of different emotions.

She smiled. "Thanks, but I can take it from here. I think I'll be okay," she said.

"Are you sure?" Lucas asked. "That was a nasty fall."

"Yeah, I'm sure," Laura replied. She pushed herself out of the bed, reaching down for her backpack. Picking it up, Laura took a step and stumbled back a bit. Lucas reached up to help her, but Laura shook her head. "I'm fine," she assured him. "Promise."

The nurse walked in from her office at that moment and shook her head.

"Oh, no you don't, Miss Paige," she said. "You sit right back down in that chair. I haven't released you just yet."

"But I'm fine!" Laura insisted.

"You are as pale as a ghost, dear," the nurse told her. "I've called your dad and excused you from your classes for the rest of the day."

She turned to Lucas and nodded. "Don't you have a class you need to be in?"

Lucas grinned sheepishly.

The nurse rolled her eyes and grabbed a sticky note. She wrote him a hall pass and sent him out of the office and to his first period class. Turning back to Laura, she smiled and took a seat on the chair next to her.

"Has this ever happened before?" the nurse asked.

"Has what ever happened before?" Laura asked back, confused.

"The fainting. Have you ever passed out before?" she repeated.

"No, ma'am," Laura answered.

"Do you know what caused it?"

Laura frowned, thinking back to what happened before the incident.

"I was just feeling really nervous," she explained. "And a little bit overwhelmed by everything around me."

The nurse nodded. "You must be under a lot of stress. I know your dad said a lot of fast changes were happening in your life." She smiled. "New family, new school, new city. A big city at that."

"My dad told you all that?" Laura asked.

She laughed. Of course, he did. Her dad was the biggest oversharer in the world, no matter what the topic was. His newest students would absolutely love him once he got started on one of his favorite stories of when he was just a young college student who thought he was on top of the world.

The nurse laughed. "He did. He loves to tell stories, doesn't he?"

Laura nodded. "That's my dad."

The nurse nodded and wrote down a few more notes.

"Just hang tight here, Miss Paige," she said, standing up. "The office will call me once your dad gets here."

She stood up and walked away, back into her office. Laura sighed and looked around the room for a bit, reading all the motivational posters that stuck onto the walls.

There were also many different types of forms hanging on bins by the wall, some for sick days and others for mental health. It was so different from any nurse's office she had ever been in. She felt at home, and it was another quiet place to get away from the noise. Laura leaned back and closed her eyes, feeling the locket hang down from around her neck.

About thirty minutes later, the nurse came out of her office. "Your dad's here," she said. "You can head down to the main office."

"Thank you," Laura said.

She picked up her bag. Pulling her phone out of her backpack, she sent a quick text to

Lucas and Shelby, asking them to get her assignments for the day and telling them that she was going home. Laura put her phone away and made her way into the office.

When she got there, her dad was nervously pacing back and forth. He relaxed the minute he saw her and ran over to give her a hug, planting a kiss on her forehead to make sure she was okay. Laura went around the counter, and her dad signed a form that allowed Laura to leave for the day, and together, they walked outside the school.

She followed her dad out into the covered parking lot to where the small blue car was parked. As she opened the door of the car, she tossed her bag into the back seat. Her dad climbed inside too, and he sighed.

"You can't scare me like that," Laura's dad said.

"I'm sorry."

"I'm just glad I didn't leave for work yet," her dad told her. "Are you sure you're okay?"

Laura smiled. "I'm okay, Dad," she said. "Everything's good. I promise!"

"Good." He started up the car and pulled out of the parking lot. Instead of turning down the road to head back home, Laura's dad drove through the city, weaving in and out of cars. "I realized we haven't been on a tour of the city yet," he announced. "I think we found the perfect day to explore."

"Don't you want to wait for Ryan and his mom?" Laura asked.

Her dad shook his head. "Nah. They don't need this. It'll just be the two of us today!"

"But what about work? What about the university?"

Laura's dad laughed. "Don't worry about that either! We don't start for another two weeks. I already told them I had a family emergency today, so they're sending me all my work later."

"I'm sorry, Dad. It's all my fault that you had to take off work," Laura apologized.

She couldn't help but feel guilty. It was her dad's first day of work, after all, and here she was, pulling him away from it.

"Don't be." He grinned and turned down a completely different road. "Today, it's just you and me. Where do you want to go first?"

"Anywhere?" Laura asked.

"Anywhere. Just give me a direction."

Laura laughed. "Alright," she said. "Left then."

For the rest of the day, Laura and her dad drove around the city. They learned all the street names, stopped to walk around the many different parks, and even discovered places for delicious ice cream, boba tea, and the biggest, messiest slice of pizza they ever saw.

Laura pointed out an outdoor marketplace hidden inside an old train station. "That looks cool!" Laura shouted.

"You're right," her dad agreed. "Let's go check it out!"

He took the next turn to get inside, finding parking just up the hill from the old train station. They walked down the street, pointing out the different art that was poking out from the walls, along with a fountain that featured a bright rainbow.

Laura laughed, watching as a few ducks waddled away from the fountain, across the street, and into the park nearby.

"We should go there next," her dad said. "Another park to check out."

"One loop around?" Laura asked.

"Absolutely!"

They laughed and continued their walk to the train station. When they made it to the marketplace, it was a chaotic mess. People ran in and out, walking up and down the stalls as they went. Laura closed her eyes, feeling overwhelmed by the scene. She reached up and tugged on her locket.

"Maybe this wasn't a good idea after all. Maybe we should just go," she told her dad.

"Are you sure?" he asked. He turned to look at her, his eyes widening as he noticed her playing with her locket. "You're right. Why don't we check out the park instead? It'll be much quieter there."

Laura nodded. Together, they crossed the street and walked around the much quieter park. They saw the same ducks and a few people out walking their dogs. When they took a seat on a bench under some willow trees near the pond, her dad looked at Laura.

"You know, Laura, when I first met your mom, she was overwhelmed by a lot of noisy places like that too, just like you."

"Really?" Laura asked.

"Yeah." He leaned back on the bench, closing his eyes. Green and blue color blobs, almost like the color of the ocean, were slowly wrapping around him. "She would always find a nice, quiet place to sit, kind of like this. I guess that's why she liked the park so much by our old house."

Laura nodded. She loved spending hours there with her mom, feeding the ducks, watching people run by, listening to the wind push through the trees. She sighed, imagining that memory once again.

She could picture her mom there, with the same green and blue colors radiating from her heart. Her mom must have been happy then too, despite knowing the inevitable. Laura smiled, looking at her dad again.

She watched the colors move around him, realizing how happy and at peace her dad was in that moment. She was getting the hang of reading emotions now, even without the help of her locket.

"Your mother was a very special woman," her dad continued. "She always knew exactly what I was feeling, and exactly how to make me feel better." He laughed and looked at Laura. "You do that too."

"I do?" Laura asked in surprise.

"Yes," he said. "Took me a long time to realize it." Turning to Laura, he picked up her hands and held them tight. "You know you can tell me anything, right?"

Laura paused. She thought about her growing worries of not being able to control her empathic powers yet, or the amount of willpower it took to even go to high school, even if it was only the second day. Emotions ran wild there, and she knew it would take a miracle to quiet her powers.

Reaching up, she rubbed her locket, wondering if there was a way to shut it all off again. Her dad watched her, smiling, waiting.

Finally, she looked at her dad. "Was Mom a lot like me?" she asked.

"She was," Laura's dad said. "You look like her more and more every day."

"What else did she do, whenever she was overwhelmed?"

Her dad thought for a moment. "She wrote in her diary a lot. She wanted me to walk next to her all the time, holding my hand as we walked through the park so she'd feel safe." He laughed. "One day, while we were feeding the ducks, she showed me the locket. Told me all about these wonderful powers she had."

Laura's ears perked up as she listened to her dad's story. This was one she hadn't heard before. She scooted closer to him, listening.

"Your mom was an empath," her dad said. "I'm sure she wrote it all down for you. That's why she gave you her locket." He smiled and turned to Laura. "You have the same powers as her, don't you?"

"I do," Laura whispered. "I found out yesterday." She sighed, feeling a huge weight slide off her shoulders and crashing to the grass beneath the bench. "School just feels like too much right now. There's so much more going on in there than I can handle."

"Is that why you passed out this morning?"

Nodding, Laura looked down at the ground.

"Hey, that's nothing to be ashamed of," her dad consoled her. "Your mom got through it, and you can too."

"I wish she was here to help me," Laura whispered. A small tear slipped down her cheek. She looked down at her shoes. "It's just so much. Everything's new, and I keep saying I'm adjusting, but I'm not."

"We'll take it one step at a time," Laura's dad said. "I'll always be here to help you." He smiled. "I helped your mom, and I can help you too."

Laura looked up at her dad. She wiped away her tears and nodded. "Are you sure?"

"I don't know much about magical powers and everything, but I know how to help my own family and those I love." He smiled. "Can I look at everything in your mother's chest so I can help you better?"

Laura thought for a moment. "Promise you won't tell anyone? Not even Cassandra?"

"I promise. Cross my heart."

Laura nodded. "Okay," she whispered. "Maybe we can look through it when we get home later."

"Perfect," Laura's dad said as he perked up. He stood up and held out his hand. "How about we do one more lap around this park, and then we look for a good place to get some dinner?"

Reaching for his hand, Laura stood up and smiled. "I think that sounds good...and delicious."

Laura and her dad walked slowly around the park. They pointed at the pond as it turned into a river, discovered a little bridge going across, and the two of them took a little shortcut.

When they arrived back at the car, Laura looked down at her locket. For once, she felt that everything was going to be okay, no matter what happened next. They took off down the road and drove around the city until the lights started to blink on one at a time. Laura looked out the window, smiling.

She was slowly feeling more at home in the new city.

Chapter Four
Blue Spirals

After about three months, with the help of her dad, Shelby, and Lucas, Laura finally managed to stabilize her life, school, and empathic powers. She managed to get through her school life fairly well, studying hard and earning her spot as an above-average student. She often had to take breaks in between classes in a quiet garden, and her teachers checked in with her from time to time.

The nurse had given all her teachers a note to make sure Laura had some quiet time for herself for at least fifteen minutes whenever she needed it. High school was getting easier to manage her powers in, and Laura learned how much she liked to create things, especially in her ceramics class.

Tara and Shelby convinced Laura to try out for the volleyball team with them. She realized it really wasn't for her, but the coach appreciated all her help and brought her on as the team manager so Laura didn't miss a single game, watching as her friends take on the other schools around and outside the city.

When Laura wasn't studying or working on school stuff, she was either with Lucas or at Shelby's house, hanging out and watching TV. They often found time to go out on hikes with the whole gang. Kyle and Tara loved surprising them with random spots outside the city, and soon, the five of them became the best of friends.

Laura loved spending every moment with her new friends and was hardly ever at home. Of course, when she wasn't with her friends, Laura practiced her powers every day with her dad in their backyard, learning how to control them without driving herself nuts.

Today had been a particularly tough day for them both.

"C'mon Laura," her dad said. "Let's try one more time, and then we gotta get some work done."

"Did you forget to grade papers?" Laura asked with a smile.

He laughed. "Not a chance. I just forgot to assign them, that's all." Laura's dad jumped up and down, shaking off his excitable emotions. He grinned. "I think you might just be about done with training after this exercise," he said.

"You really think so?"

"Absolutely." He beamed. "Of course, I still like spending time with you, so we'll keep practicing every day." He paused. "Actually, I have an even better idea for our final training day."

"What's that?" Laura asked.

"A surprise for later," he said with a smile. "Alright, Laura, give me the worst emotion you can think of!" He was still grinning eagerly, bouncing up and down.

She wondered what her dad was up to but shook her head. She took a stance and breathed in and out, thinking of what emotion to give her dad. Laura didn't want him to be too sad today, but he was already so excited. She wondered if there was a way to calm him down.

Laura shook her head. No. That was way too easy. If anything, Laura needed a challenge today. Something big, something she had never made her father feel before. Her eyes flew open, and her fingertips turned red.

"Are you sure you're ready for this, Dad?" Laura called out.

"I'm ready for anything!" he shouted.

"Alright then." Laura smiled.

She charged at her dad, fingertips glowing a brighter red as she approached him. With just a single tap, she touched his shoulder and took a few steps back, watching her dad carefully.

His smile slipped away, and his eyebrows furrowed in anger. He looked at Laura and snapped, "Laura Abigail Paige, you take this away right now!"

Laura broke into a big grin. She tapped her dad on the shoulder again, taking away his anger. Gleefulness and pride soared into his heart, and he pulled Laura into a tight hug.

"You did it!" he cried. "You're a real empath now!"

"Thanks, Dad," Laura whispered, breaking away from his embrace. "I'm sorry," she said quietly.

"Why?"

"I've never seen you so angry before," Laura explained. "I didn't want to do it, but I thought it would be a good challenge."

Her dad laughed. "That *was* a scary feeling." He sat down on the back porch steps. "I do get angry sometimes, but I always choose to feel something else instead. I never want to be angry at anyone I love, no matter what happens." He smiled. "Don't worry, you'll never make me feel like that again."

Laura smiled too. "Thanks, Dad," she whispered again.

"How about we celebrate with a home-cooked meal?" he asked. "One of your mother's best recipes."

"Are we cooking together?" Laura asked.

"We'll get it ready for your stepmom and brother," he said. "Let's go get washed up."

She nodded, and her dad helped her to her feet. As they walked inside and washed their hands at the sink, Laura wondered if there were more her powers could do.

She pulled out a few ingredients while her dad looked at the recipes, choosing one of their favorites. He hid the box away at the back of the pantry, and they started to prepare the soup.

While she cut up the vegetables, Laura wondered if school would be much easier if she used her powers. She smiled. Maybe now, she could help others around her at school and would no longer need her quiet time.

The four of them eventually sat down at the table and enjoyed a delicious meal of minestrone soup and a pot roast. They talked about their day and what they were looking forward to that week. Ryan seemed to be in a bit of trouble, but he didn't elaborate or explain much.

When they finished dinner, Laura sat up and stretched.

"I'll get the dishes tonight," she told Ryan. "Don't worry about it."

Ryan looked at her suspiciously. "You sure?" he asked.

"Yeah," Laura said with a smile. "We can team up tomorrow."

"Whatever," Ryan said.

He turned and left the dining room, leaving a pile of dishes behind him. Laura shrugged and collected them all. As she washed the plates, bowls, and pots, Laura formed her plan in her mind for school.

Friday was usually full of happiness since everyone was excited for the weekend to come. Especially with this weekend, they would end up having three days off due to a holiday. She grinned. This was the perfect time to put her plan into action.

Anyone she saw as sad or tired, she would remind them with her powers about the break that was coming soon.

Laura dried off the final plate and put it away. She said goodnight to her parents and ran upstairs to her bedroom. Closing the door behind her, Laura dug around in her chest, looking for the perfect notes to help her pull off her master plan.

She sat down at her desk and pulled open her diary, writing about her day, growing more and more excited about her magical plan that was sure to work. Her homework laid forgotten inside her backpack. She was too excited to care.

***

The next morning, Laura's alarm went off. She gasped and shot up from her desk. She had dozed off on top of her notebook while trying to organize her notes. "Shoot," she whispered, pulling out her homework, working on it as quickly as she could for her first period class. Everything else, she could get away with doing later. She usually did most of her homework during lunch anyway.

Laura shoved the folders into her backpack, scrambled around her room, pulling on whatever clothes she could find, and quickly dashed down the stairs. She grabbed a bagel off the kitchen counter and shoved it in her mouth before throwing her shoes on.

"Going a little fast there?" Cassandra asked, sipping her cup of coffee in the kitchen.

"Woke up late," Laura explained. "Is the bus here yet?"

"Ryan's waiting outside," she replied. "You have plenty of time!"

"Thanks!" Laura called.

She rushed out the door, bumping into Ryan, who was waiting on the steps.

Ryan scowled. "Took you long enough."

"I'm sorry," she apologized. "I can't believe I woke up late. I usually always wake up before my alarm does."

Laura and Ryan walked up to the bus stop, waiting as the blue bus rounded the corner. They boarded the bus and found their usual spots. Shelby hopped on at the next stop, and the two girls excitedly talked about their weekend plans.

Ryan, who was sitting behind them, groaned. He always found their girl talk annoying and would slap his headphones on to tune them out. Laura and Shelby turned around.

"Can I help you?" Shelby asked.

"Yes," Ryan said. "Can you please shut up about the weekend? Literally, no one cares."

Shelby gasped. Laura turned on her brother, her tone stern and angry.

"Don't talk to my friend like that," she snapped. "Why don't you just listen to your music and let us be excited for the weekend?"

"Imagine being excited for a three-day weekend," Ryan said with a smirk. "So lame."

He turned and faced the window, pulling his hood up and putting his headphones over his ears, ignoring Laura and Shelby.

Laura turned back to Shelby. "Ignore him," she said. "I'm sorry. He's been in a bad mood lately."

"Seems like it," Shelby said.

They continued their conversation, talking about visiting the big and beautiful new park near the mountains, where the observatory was. Lucas, Tara, and Kyle were all going with them. They were going to spend the night under the stars, camping, and leaving as much school talk out of it as possible.

Laura grinned. She couldn't wait to share this excitement with the others at school.

When the bus pulled up to the school, Ryan was the first one to get off. He shoved past Laura and Shelby, as well as the other students on the bus, still wearing his headphones. Laura sighed and turned to Shelby.

"I'll meet you in the Hub before our first class, okay?" she said. "I need to take care of something!"

"Sure," Shelby said. She smiled. "Don't be late, okay? I hate it when I have to stand there all alone. People always stare and laugh at me when I do. I don't want to look like a fool again."

"No promises," Laura said.

She laughed and took off in another direction. She pushed through the sea of students, spotting a few younger kids talking by the art room. One of them had spilled their art supplies everywhere, and when she went down to pick them up, Laura dove down to help.

"Thanks," the girl said.

"No problem." Laura smiled.

She let her hand brush against the girl's briefly, and in that instant, she sent a spark of excitement to the girl.

Once everything was picked up, Laura walked away, listening as the girl said, "Is it just me, or is today going to be a really good day?"

Laura grinned. She wandered down the hallways, continuing her mission, looking for other students who looked sad or needed a little pick-me-up. The more she met, the more she realized her excitement was growing.

Everyone's emotions weren't as overwhelming now, and although she could still feel them, she didn't have to worry about passing out in the middle of class anymore. Laura happily skipped to the Hub, finding Shelby by the lockers. As Laura opened up her locker, she turned to Shelby.

"Don't you think today's going to just be amazing?" she asked.

Shelby laughed. "Sure," she said. "It's just another Friday."

Lucas joined them at their lockers. He looked around the Hub and grinned. "Is it just me, or does everyone seem really happy today?"

"Just you," Shelby said.

"No idea what you're talking about," Laura said with a smile.

The bell rang, and Laura grabbed Shelby's hand, sending another burst of joyful energy to her best friend.

"See you later, Lucas," she cried. "We have a class to catch!"

As Laura and Shelby ran to their class, Laura looked around at the other students. Everyone was slowly growing into a better mood. She smiled.

Happiness was contagious, despite what people thought. Shelby and Laura took their seats in their class.

"I heard we're watching a movie today," Shelby whispered. "Sounds like a good start to a Friday, right?"

"Absolutely," Laura whispered back.

She turned her attention to the front of the room. But it wasn't the teacher's attention that caught her eye; it was someone else's.

One of the students at the front of the room didn't have the yellow sparks she had seen on everyone else. Instead, blue spirals dripped down from him, and he laid his head down on the desk.

Laura frowned. She thought everyone was feeling better today, but then again, something else felt completely off. This wasn't a normal kind of sadness, but one that something else had brought on. Laura was distracted the whole period, wondering who could do such a thing.

As they walked to their next class, Shelby looked at Laura.

"Everything okay?" she asked. "You seemed kind of distracted back there."

"Yeah," Laura said. "I'm fine." She smiled. "Nothing to worry about here!"

"Alright...," Shelby said, sounding unconvinced.

The more they walked through the school, the more and more sad and miserable faces Laura saw. She overheard a group of friends canceling their plans for the weekend, and others grew extremely quiet and withdrawn.

Someone had to be doing this, Laura thought.

She looked around for the source of what could've caused something like this but couldn't find anyone else. For the first time since Laura discovered her powers, she realized she couldn't be the only one out there. There had to be another empath in the school who was bringing everyone's moods down.

During the rest of her classes, Laura was distracted. She continued to doodle absentmindedly in her notebooks, unsure of what would happen next. More and more students became sad, and the whole happy vibe the school had that morning had completely disappeared by lunchtime.

At least Shelby was still in a good mood, and Lucas seemed unaffected as well. As they left fourth period, Shelby stood up and stretched.

"I left something in my locker," she said. "I'll meet you outside."

"We'll be in the middle garden, like always," Laura said with a smile.

She watched her friend walk away. Laura was a little worried that the sadness that was spreading to the school would eventually catch on, and for a moment, she hoped Shelby wouldn't lose her spark today.

Laura shook her head and skipped happily to the cafeteria, a few people shooting her dirty looks as she did. She tried her best to send out more happy and positive emotions as she made her way to the cafeteria, but it was harder to do, now that there were more people around.

Laura got her lunch and walked out to the garden where Lucas, Tara, and Kyle were already sitting. Tara was surrounded by the blue swirls too, and as Laura took a seat on the bench, she looked at her friend.

"Tara, are you feeling okay?"

"Not really," Tara mumbled. "Nothing seems exciting to me anymore. I just want to crawl in bed and sleep all day."

"Why?" Kyle asked. "You were super excited all week about this camping trip!"

Tara shook her head. "Just the thought of having fun makes me even sadder."

Lucas sighed. "I don't know what happened," he said. "One minute, everyone's ready to go and enjoy their long weekend, and now, we're here, like rain clouds just appeared over everyone's heads and rinsed the joy out."

"Good simile," Laura said. "They're more like blue spirals."

"What?"

Laura blinked. "I said, that was a good simile," she corrected herself with a nervous laugh.

Laura sat down next to Tara and gave her a hug, sending the happiest thoughts and emotions she could conjure to her friend.

"Don't worry, Tara," Laura assured her. "We'll have the most fantastic weekend ever!"

Some of the blue faded away as she hugged Tara, but not enough. Still, it was enough to get a small smile out of Tara. Laura nodded, and they dug into their meals of pizza and salad. Shelby still hadn't joined them, and both Lucas and Laura looked at each other as lunch came to an end.

"We'll see you guys after school," Lucas said as he and Laura stood up. "Just to confirm all our plans for this weekend."

"Sure," Kyle nodded. "Don't let the bad vibes bite!"

He winked, and he and Tara took off in another direction.

Lucas and Laura began walking to their next class when they found Shelby sitting at a table in the almost-empty cafeteria. Laura gasped, seeing her best friend covered completely by the blue swirls.

"Shelby!" Laura cried. "Are you alright? What happened?"

"Not really," Shelby pouted. "I was so excited to see you guys at lunch," she said.

"But when I went to grab my food, I bumped into your stepbrother. Now, I just feel like I want to sleep forever."

Laura frowned. She sat down next to Shelby, her mind racing. Could Ryan be behind this? It wasn't possible. But he seemed the grumpiest this morning on the bus. Maybe he *was* behind it.

As their ceramics class started, Laura knew she had to confront her brother when she got home. She just had to know what was going on.

Chapter Five
Stolen Happiness

The day came and went, and by the end of it, everyone was tired and ready to go home. Lucas looked around at his friends.

"Come on, gang," he cheered. "Our camping trip will cheer us up!"

"Whatever you say," Kyle murmured with a yawn.

Shelby and Tara only shrugged.

Laura smiled. "Don't worry, we *will* have fun. Just you wait!"

They agreed to meet outside Lucas' house in a few hours, no matter what they were feeling like, and Laura and Shelby boarded the bus home. Ryan was nowhere to be seen. As they took their seats, the bus driver looked back at all the students.

"Rough day?" she asked.

"You could say that," Laura answered.

The bus driver nodded. She turned back to face the road, closed the doors, and took off down the street. Laura stared out the window, wondering how she was going to talk to Ryan when she got home. She practiced the words over and over in her head, but nothing seemed good enough.

When they arrived in her neighborhood, Shelby said a sad goodbye to Laura and jumped off the bus. Laura hopped off too, walking the rest of the way. She stopped, noticing her dad in the driveway.

"Oh, no," she mumbled. "I forgot about the final test!"

"Ready to go, Laura?" her dad shouted, swinging the keys around his finger.

Sighing, Laura looked at her dad. "Not today," she mumbled again. "I had a pretty rough day at school."

"What happened?"

Laura looked around and started to explain her day. She told him all about the sadness running rampant through the school, even though she tried her best to get everyone excited for the weekend. She told him how even her closest friends were affected by the sadness.

"It was too much for me to fix," Laura said quietly. "What if my powers just stopped working?"

"Nonsense," her dad said. "C'mon, let's go inside. I'll pour you some tea."

Following her dad inside the house, Laura tugged on her locket. She took a seat at the kitchen counter, letting her feet dangle. Her dad set a glass of sweet tea in front of her, and she smiled, sipping on it, listening to her dad tell her all about his day at the university. He was going on and on about a few of his students and their exciting class discussion.

"You would love this class, Laura. Psychology just brings out the best and most interesting characters!"

Laura grinned. "Sounds like a great class today."

"It was!" he laughed. "I can't wait to tell Cassandra also when she gets home."

"Ryan hasn't come home yet, has he?" Laura asked, looking around.

She didn't see her stepbrother's bag on the ground, nor his shoes by the front door. Usually, it meant he was still out and about, doing what, she had no idea. Maybe causing more and more chaos. She shook her head. There was no way Ryan was behind this.

"Not yet," her dad replied. "Haven't seen him all week besides during dinner. He's just a quiet kid, doesn't like to be bothered." He smiled. "As long as he's home every night, I'll be fine."

Laura nodded and stretched. "I'm gonna head upstairs," she said. "Thanks for listening, Dad."

She smiled and hopped off the chair. She gave him a big hug and ran down the hall. With each step, her locket bounced off her chest, flashing between the yellow and blue gems. Laura sighed and crashed onto her bed, staring at the ceiling for a few minutes, just relaxing her mind from the day.

She grabbed her journal and made a list of all the emotions she felt that day that were hers, along with any that she felt from others. It was one of the few exercises her mom had written down for her, and Laura found it the most helpful.

Once she was done, she rolled off her bed and started to pack up her things for the camping trip. Although they wouldn't be going outside the city, Laura still packed some of her old camping gear. She tucked her black and yellow sleeping bag off to the side, grabbed her flashlight and a few batteries, and finally, all of her outdoor clothing for the weekend.

Laura always made sure she was prepared, unsure about what kinds of things they would see out in the wild. Better to be over-prepared than under. Lucas had told her it was a different kind of camping, but she didn't quite know what that meant. So, of course, she had to have a solution for any possible obstacle.

Laura set her duffle bag next to her sleeping bag and stretched. She tied her hair into braids and shot a few finger guns at herself, grinning. Her smile slipped away when her eyes landed on her locket.

She played with it carefully, wondering whether it would be fine to leave it at home for the weekend. Laura hardly ever took it off, except to shower, swim, or when she was sleeping. But it was always nearby, ready for her to put back on. She thought for a moment, debating whether to leave it at home or not.

After a few minutes, Laura finally took it off. She hid it in her drawer and patted it softly. She didn't want to lose it while they were out in the woods and climbing mountains, doing who knows what at the campsite. Finally, she was ready to go. Laura grabbed her things, raced down the stairs, and grabbed an apple.

"Bye, Dad," she said, giving him a quick hug. "I'll see you on Monday, okay?"

"Don't have too much fun without me!" her dad called out. "Wait, Laura, do you have your keys?"

"Yes."

"Bus pass?"

"Yes, Dad."

"Camping gear?"

"Yes!" Laura grinned. "I have everything! I promise, I'll be fine. I'll be with my friends the entire time."

"I know, I know," her dad chuckled. "Stay safe. I want you back here all in one piece!"

Laura rolled her eyes and laughed. Opening the door, she pushed her way through and stepped out onto the lawn. She walked down the sidewalk and to the curb, taking in a deep breath of the crisp autumn air.

It was going to be a great weekend, no matter what happened. She made her way down to the bus stop, catching Ryan on his way back.

"Where have *you* been all day?" Laura asked.

Ryan shrugged. "Out and about. What's it to you?"

"Nothing, just worried," Laura said.

He looked her up and down, a slight smile forming on his lips. "Are you heading off on that grand weekend you couldn't shut up about earlier today?"

"Yes, I am, and it's going to be great," Laura said. "What are you doing this weekend?"

"Nothing," Ryan said. "You missed the bus, by the way."

He turned around and walked up the street towards their house. He had a little skip in his step, and Laura shook her head. She turned away from him and made her way down the street towards the bus stop.

Taking a seat on the bench, Laura looked around, watching as other cars and taxis drove by. She smiled, glad that they lived on the outskirts of the city. It was just enough like her old home that Laura didn't mind it too much.

She looked on as her neighbors walked by, a few emotional spirals swirling off of them. Some people were tired while others excited, and most were just content with their day.

Finally, the bus pulled up. At this late in the afternoon, a lot of men and women got off, all dressed in business clothes. They all said hello to her as they stepped off, and Laura waited until the last person was gone. She stepped on, scanned her pass, and took a seat.

The bus stayed for a few minutes longer, and when a few other people got on, it took off down the road. It passed by Shelby's street, and Shelby jumped on board, carrying a sleeping bag, a backpack, and a tent. She smiled.

"Are you feeling better?" Laura asked, happy to see her friend's smile.

"Absolutely." Shelby put her bag down. "I just remembered how excited I was for this trip."

"Me too," Laura chimed.

The bus took off again, and Laura looked out the window. They passed by the tall skyscrapers and other cars in the setting sunlight. There were a few cars honking as people strolled down the sidewalks.

The bus tumbled on slowly through the city, Laura watching as people passed by outside. The entire ride to Lucas' street, Shelby eagerly talked about all the things she wanted to do at the campsite.

"Do you think we'll roast marshmallows?" she asked.

Laura shrugged.

"I haven't had a s'more since I was little," she said. "Mom used to make the best ones."

"My dad makes some pretty good ones too," Laura said with a laugh. "We should compare recipes!"

"That would be amazing," Shelby agreed.

The bus pulled up to their stop, and the two teens hopped off the bus with their sleeping bags and tents. They walked down the street to the apartment complex near the school and waited inside the lobby. The doorman waved and smiled at the girls.

"Hey, girls. Waiting for Lucas?" he asked.

"Yes, sir," Laura said with a grin.

"I'll let him know you're here." The doorman picked up a phone and spoke softly for a moment before hanging up the receiver. "He said he'll be down soon!"

"Thanks!" Shelby said.

Tara and Kyle came inside the apartment lobby too. Kyle grinned.

"Wow, you guys are all packed up and ready to go!"

"Where's Lucas?" Tara asked.

"On his way down," Laura replied.

She grinned, looking at the excitement just popping off of her friends. At least they weren't as sad as they had been earlier.

Finally, Lucas came down in the elevator. He grinned. "Come on, guys," he said. "My car is parked just outside!"

The five of them loaded their things in his car and piled into the seats. Laura somehow ended up in the passenger seat, leaving Shelby, Kyle, and Tara all squished in the back. They all made sure to push her to take that seat, and she wasn't sure why. Lucas grinned and started up the car.

They drove through the city, taking a few twists and turns, until finally, the buildings started to fade away and turn into the mountains that surrounded the city.

Laura smiled. It reminded her so much of her old town, surrounded by trees. They started to climb the mountain, winding in and out of the roads. They passed a few other cars that were coming down the mountain on the narrow road, everyone, but Lucas, enjoying the magnificent view.

The sun started to set early, and Lucas pulled up into the parking spot just in time. The old observatory was overgrown, but there were a few astronomers pulling up and running inside the building. Lucas led the way, and the four of them followed him to a small area in the forest. Laura could only see the mountains and the trees that stretched for miles on the horizon.

"It's so pretty," Laura whispered.

"Oh, this isn't even the best view," Lucas said with a grin.

Tara rolled her eyes. "Lucas never shows anyone his secret spot. We've been begging him for years."

Lucas winked at Laura. "Sorry, Tara," he said. "I'll only show it to the most special person in the entire world. It's my secret!"

Kyle laughed. "Sure," he said. "Tell me when you find that special person because you seem to have the worst luck in that department."

Everyone laughed. Soon, they got to work, setting up their campsite. Kyle gathered up wood for their fire while Shelby and Tara spread out all their sleeping bags and tents. They hung up a tarp over the tents as well, just in case it started to rain. Lucas tied their bags of food up in the trees to avoid attracting animals, while Laura unpacked the car and brought over all their supplies.

Once the campsite was done, the five of them climbed up a hill, watching the last bit of sunlight disappear behind the mountains. Laura looked around at her friends, feeling the peace that was coming from them.

Not just happiness or excitement, but a feeling of peace. She closed her eyes, feeling it too. It was one of her favorite feelings in the world.

As they hiked back down, both Lucas and Kyle had forgotten their flashlights. The boys stumbled in the dark behind the girls, while Laura laughed and tossed them a spare one she had in her pocket.

When they made it back to the campsite, Laura showed off her cooking skills, a recipe that she learned from her dad during all the times they went camping together. She dished out the hot dogs and soup, and everyone sat around the fire.

"This is the best meal I've ever eaten!" Kyle exclaimed as he scarfed down his bowl of soup.

"Way better than what you made last year, Lucas," Tara added, biting into her hot dog.

"Hey, I tried my best," Lucas argued back. "We're just lucky we met Laura!"

Laura blushed. She looked down at her own plate of food and picked slowly at it, savoring every flavor that was in the broth.

When everyone finished their dinner, Kyle pulled out his guitar and started to serenade the group, his voice equally as amazing as his musical talent.

Laura looked over at Lucas, and for the first time, she saw him differently. It wasn't because of the fire sparks flickering in front of him. No, it was something else, something different.

Kyle sang a few more songs, and then they shifted into telling scary stories with s'mores. They gobbled up the s'mores, laughing, and telling other stories from when they were younger, before they all knew each other.

Finally, they fell asleep under the stars. Laura was the last one awake, staring up at the stars high above them. She smiled, hoping her mom was watching them from the house in the clouds.

***

Laura waved goodbye to Lucas as he dropped her off at her house. He grinned, "see you at school tomorrow!"

Laura nodded, a goofy smile still crossing her face. When Lucas drove off, Laura ran inside, her heart skipping a beat for a second. Why did she feel like this? Nothing made any sense at all! She dropped her bag of dirty clothes off in the washing machine and looked around the house.

"I'm home!" she called out. "Anyone here?"

"Just me," Ryan answered. He turned the corner, swinging Laura's locket around on his finger. "This is a pretty nifty tool you got here," he said. "Didn't realize there was another empath in the house. Until you tried to take my sadness away the other day." He smiled.

"What are you doing?" Laura demanded. "Give that back!"

"Nah," Ryan said. "I think I'll hold onto it a little longer." He grinned. "Oh, and these as well."

He reached forward, grabbing Laura's arm. It was like a wave crashing over her, and one by one, Laura could feel all of her emotions leaving.

Everything from hope to sadness to happiness and whatever she was feeling about Lucas. Ryan held the swirl of colors in his hand and tucked them inside his locket.

"Thanks for your help, sis," Ryan chuckled. "Can't wait to make the rest of the city feel what I feel!"

"Wait," Laura called out weakly. "You can't do that!"

"Oh, I can, and I will," Ryan said. "See you tomorrow!"

Laura's soulless body sank to the floor, unsure of what to feel. She wasn't sad or scared, just empty. She couldn't feel anything. Tears couldn't even fall from her eyes, and she watched as her stepbrother ran out the door. All she could feel was emptiness.

Chapter Six
Bringing Laura Back

A week later, Laura rolled over in her bed. She didn't feel like getting up or going to school. She tried her best, but nothing felt the same anymore. She started to drift away from her friends, who came by after school to check on her. Her dad grew worried about his daughter, and soon, the rest of the city slowly became sadder and sadder.

Laura wasn't out there to help people. She just didn't care anymore; she didn't even have an ounce of happiness left in her to share. And Ryan was out there, spreading his negative emotions with her locket.

One evening, Laura managed to get herself out of bed. Someone was knocking on the door downstairs, so she slowly made her way down the steps. Opening the door, Laura stared blankly at her friends' faces. Shelby and Lucas were there, looking at her with worried looks.

"We brought your homework," Shelby said. "The teachers said you don't have to do it just yet. Whenever you're ready."

"Thanks," Laura muttered.

"We miss you, Laura," Lucas whispered. "Can we hang out for a bit?"

"I guess," Laura muttered again.

She stepped out of the way and let Lucas and Shelby come inside. They took a seat on the couch while Laura sat on the chair. The clock ticked as the three of them stared at each other.

"Okay, that's it. I'm just going to say it," Shelby announced as she broke the awkward silence. "Laura, what happened? Why are you acting so weird?"

"We're worried sick about you," Lucas added. "I've been depressed before, but this is worse than anything I've ever experienced. This came too quickly. You were cheerful and happy just last week."

"I'm fine," Laura said flatly. "Just fine."

"No, you're not," Shelby snapped. "I miss my best friend. I miss *you*."

Laura's heart skipped a beat. Shelby really thought of her as her best friend? Laura never had a best friend before. For a moment, she felt like smiling. But the lack of emotions inside her snuffed out the light, and the fleeting moment escaped. She looked down at the ground, unsure of what to say.

"Laura," Lucas said. "I know the real you is in there somewhere. You just have to find her and pull her out."

She glanced up at him. "How do you know that?"

"I just saw it," he explained. "Just for a moment." Lucas smiled. "Whatever happened to you, it's just hiding there, trying to fight back."

Laura shrugged. How could her own feelings just fight back? Everything was just too overwhelming. Anything she thought she could feel went back down and under the black sludge slowly filling her up.

Ryan poisoned her. She could feel everything he felt before, and for a moment, she understood her stepbrother.

Shelby and Lucas stayed for the rest of the night until her family came home. They made dinner, watched movies, and hung out, despite how low and apathetic Laura was feeling. She did feel a bit better when her friends were there with her though.

So, they continued this pattern over the next few weeks, either both of them visiting her or taking turns. Shelby brought all the notes and homework for Laura and worked on them with her whenever they could, and she would fill her in on all the drama that had been happening around the school lately.

"There's been more fights than ever," Shelby explained. "The teachers have no idea what went wrong. Everyone seemed so happy just a couple weeks ago. Now, they seem to all hate each other."

Laura really wanted to tell her best friend about her powers, but she couldn't. It was all her fault that the school, and probably the city, was falling apart. Laura wanted to be out there, helping others find their happiness again, but she barely wanted to help herself.

She was drowning in the darkness with no hope for escape. Whenever they finished their work and had some free time before Shelby had to go home for dinner, Shelby would either turn on the television or put on their favorite song, and the two of them would dance around, just being silly without a care in the world.

For a moment, Laura felt happy. But the happiness didn't stay long and was once again snuffed out after Shelby left.

Whenever Lucas came on his own, they would sit out in the backyard on a picnic blanket and just talk. Laura often found herself talking a lot with Lucas, but she never knew why. They spent all their time together, reading books or watching movies.

Sometimes, the rare times Laura let out a laugh, she'd catch Lucas just staring at her, his eyes sparkling in the sunlight.

"What?" she asked.

Lucas shook his head. "Nothing," he said. "Just caught up in the moment."

Laura's heart skipped another beat. A small smile appeared, but then it faded away quickly. Lucas always managed to bring back something, but just like with Shelby, it was always something that Laura couldn't exactly pin-point. And it wouldn't stay for long either. Lucas always made sure to give her a hug before he left.

"I'll see you tomorrow, alright?"

Laura nodded. She watched him leave, touching her heart.

"What is wrong with you?" she whispered to herself.

***

Finally, the weekend soon arrived. Lucas and Shelby showed up to Laura's house Saturday morning, telling her how many students were absent from school now.

"There's hardly anyone on campus anymore. The principal made this huge announcement that a lot of parents have been taking their kids out and letting them stay at home instead," Shelby said. "Something's definitely going around. Maybe it's the flu or some sort of illness?"

"I've been calling it the *Great City Depression*," Lucas said. He cracked a smile, but it slipped away. "It hasn't caught on yet. It's getting really tiring seeing so many sad faces around. Makes me feel sad too."

"What does it feel like?" Laura asked.

"Like I could curl up under my blanket and cry all day," Shelby explained. "I don't want to do anything, and there's this feeling that something is missing in my life. I can't really explain what it is though."

"Or someone," Lucas added. "I feel that too. But it's not as overwhelming."

Laura frowned. "I haven't really felt that," she said.

"It's so strange," Shelby whispered. She sighed. "Anyway, what movie are we watching today?"

Laura shrugged. She led them into the living room. Her parents were out for the day, and Ryan was still sleeping upstairs. She tried her best to avoid her stepbrother, who seemed to be in a much better mood lately. He spent every moment with her, asking her how she was feeling in the most mocking way, dangling her locket in front of her face.

Laura never felt like taking it back, and even if she tried, Ryan would just douse her with his sadness once again. One day, she would talk to him. She wasn't sure what she would say or how she would even approach him, but one day.

The three of them took their seats on the couch, and Lucas flipped through the channels to try and find something appealing, settling on a cute, lighthearted movie. He stretched his arm around Laura and pulled her close, giving her a light kiss on her forehead.

"You're going to be okay, I promise. You're safe with me," he whispered softly.

She leaned into him as if on auto-pilot, not knowing why this felt so comfortable. Shelby looked over at them and smiled before jumping up.

"I'll make some popcorn!" she cried.

Shelby raced out of the room and into the kitchen. The movie continued to play, but Laura wasn't paying attention. She turned her gaze to Lucas, watching him laugh at some silly joke on the screen. The happy feeling inside her started to come back but was doused once again. She loved listening to his laugh. It sounded so peaceful and made her want to smile.

Laura turned back to the television, watching the cartoon characters skip across the screen. Shelby returned shortly with a big bowl of popcorn and set it on Laura's lap.

"Will you be the popcorn holder?" Shelby asked with a smile.

"Sure," Laura said.

She *was* sitting in the middle, after all. They continued to watch the movie.

When the credits finally started to roll, Shelby's cell phone went off. She picked it up and left the room, leaving Lucas and Laura alone for the time being.

When Shelby returned, she sighed. "I have to go, guys," she said. "I'll be back tomorrow." Shelby smiled. "I refuse to give up on you, Laura. I will do everything I can to make you feel better."

"Sure, okay. See you tomorrow," Laura mumbled.

Shelby nodded and said goodbye. Once she left, Lucas stood up.

"That's it," he said. He held out his hand. "Come on, we're getting you out of this house."

"I don't want to go," Laura declined. "I want to stay right here."

"Nope. You and I are going outside together."

Laura sighed and reluctantly reached out her hand to grab his. He pulled her to her feet and led Laura out the front door to his car. Lucas opened the car door on the passenger side, and Laura got in. Lucas slightly smiled the whole way to his side and jumped into the driver's seat. He turned on his radio, and soft music played.

As they drove through the city, Laura looked around. It was no longer the bright, happy place she saw when she moved in. Everything seemed so gray and dismal.

"Where are we going?" Laura asked.

"It's a surprise," Lucas said.

He drove right out of the city and into the nearby forest. He turned right, leading up to the observatory, and then turned left down a different route. They climbed higher and higher up the mountains.

When they finally came to a stop, Lucas parked in a gravel lot. He ran around to the other side and opened the door for Laura, smiling from ear to ear. At least he still hadn't lost the twinkle in his eye or the sparkle in his smile.

Laura decided to trust him and stepped out of the car. Lucas grabbed her hand.

"Close your eyes," he said. "I'll lead you there, okay?"

"Okay," Laura replied, still unsure of what was going on.

She closed her eyes and held onto his hand.

Lucas led Laura up a hiking path with instructions as they walked.

"Watch your step," he said. "There's a branch to your right."

He pulled her away from a boulder and carefully guided her across a trickling brook. She could hear the birds chirping above her and the water rushing below her. Laura clutched his hand tighter.

"Don't worry," he assured her. "I've got you."

"How much more hiking are we going to do? My legs are starting to hurt," Laura asked.

"We're almost there," Lucas said. "Just one more path to climb."

They pushed through the trees for a few more minutes, until finally, Lucas laughed.

"Alright, Laura," he whispered. "Open your eyes."

Laura's eyes fluttered open, and she looked around. They were standing on a small clearing, higher than the other hills at the campsite. Trees around them were strung with little solar panel lanterns that slowly lit up.

On the edge of the cliff, there was a bench swing, swaying against the autumn breeze. Lucas grinned and gestured his hand towards the swing.

Laura stared at the little picturesque scene for just a little longer.

"Wow," she whispered.

"Right?" Lucas exclaimed. He grinned and took a seat on the bench swing. "This isn't even the best part." He patted the empty spot next to him.

Laura sat down beside him. She followed his gaze to the overlook and looked down. She gasped. The sun was setting just over the city, and one by one, lights lit on under the golden sunlight. A golden ray ignited the entire city, and the sunlight glinted off skyscrapers and cars.

Lucas smiled. "Welcome to my secret spot," he announced.

"This is your secret spot?" Laura asked, surprised. "I was expecting something else!"

Lucas laughed. "There she is," he said. "What were you expecting?"

"I don't know," Laura admitted. "Maybe a field of flowers or something."

She smiled wholeheartedly for the first time in several weeks and turned to look at the city once more. For the first time in a long time, Laura felt a sense of peacefulness.

"It's beautiful," she whispered.

"Flowers?" Lucas repeated with a laugh. "I wasn't expecting that!" He set his hand down on top of hers. "I come here whenever I need to blow off steam," he said. "Or when

I just want to be by myself. Promise you won't tell anyone?"

"Cross my heart. Do you come here a lot?" Laura asked.

"Whenever I can," Lucas explained. "It's always pretty, day or night, but this time of day feels so magical. Just perfect."

"It does!" Laura agreed. She smiled, but it quickly slipped away. She turned to look at Lucas. "I thought you said you wouldn't bring just anyone here? Just the one special person?" Laura asked, remembering their conversation by the campfire.

"You're not just anyone," Lucas said. He leaned over and kissed her on the lips.

Laura's heart skipped a beat again. She could feel something deep within her, fighting back. The dark emotions inside her couldn't strike the light away. She turned to look at Lucas, and slowly, a small smile appeared on her face.

"What was that for?" she asked.

Lucas smiled, his eyes sparkling. "I think I love you, Laura," he whispered. "You *are* the one special person to me."

Laura's heart beat even faster, the light growing bigger inside her. She wasn't sure how to answer, but the longer she looked at him, the more she couldn't keep it in anymore.

"I think I love you too," she said in one breath. "You're amazing." She smiled, but once again, it faded away. "You didn't just bring me out here to tell me that, did you?"

"That was part of it," Lucas said. "I've been wanting to tell you that since the day I met you."

Laura blushed, and she looked down at her feet.

"But you're right. I have another reason," Lucas added. "What's holding you down? This is not the Laura I fell in love with, and I want her back."

Laura sighed and turned back to look at the city. She shook her head, and finally, turned to Lucas.

"Can you keep a secret?" she asked nervously.

"Only if you keep mine," Lucas said.

Nodding, Laura told him everything. She told him about her powers, her stepbrother, and how he took away all of her emotions. She didn't stop talking until she finished her story. Lucas listened, nodding intently.

When she finally finished, Laura looked at Lucas. "I don't know what I'm going to do next."

"I think we should get that locket back," Lucas suggested. "If that's what's causing all this, then that will be what fixes it."

"You're right," Laura said. She squeezed his hand. "What do we do?"

Lucas sighed. He turned to look at the city too, before turning back to give Laura another kiss. "I think you and I need to enjoy this moment for just a little longer before we think about anything else."

Laura nodded, her smile growing bigger. She leaned up against Lucas, and they spent the next hour there, looking at the city and the stars above them, arms wrapped around each other.

When it was finally time for them to leave, Lucas and Laura made their way back down to the car. This time, Laura got to see the trail. It was even more beautiful than the sounds she heard. She could feel it all around her, and here, far away from the city, she felt calm and almost happy again. Laura didn't want to go back home yet, but she knew she had to.

They climbed into the car, and Laura stared out the window. She gasped, looking at the black and blue cloud circling the city, falling down around it like a dome of sadness.

"Do you see that?" she asked.

"See what?" Lucas asked back.

Laura described it to him, her eyes widening as they grew closer and closer to the big bubble.

She turned to Lucas and said, "When we get into the city, you might feel a wave of sadness surrounding you. Whatever you do, try to fight it, and don't let it get to you."

He reached over and grabbed her hand. "No matter what happens, I'll be here for you, always."

"Me too." Laura grinned.

They held hands as Lucas drove closer and closer towards the bubble. They passed through it without too much trouble, but even then, Laura could feel whatever happiness she had earlier slowly disappearing. She looked over at Lucas and noticed a single tear rolling down his cheek. He looked back at her, a forced smile still strong on his face.

"See, I'm fine," he said. "I love you so much."

"I love you too," Laura said back.

She looked at him, seeing the smile on his face slowly fighting away the despair and misery. Lucas was much stronger than she would've ever thought, and in that moment, she knew they would be okay.

Chapter Seven
Discovering Ryan's Secret

When Laura got home, she pushed the door open.

"Hello?" she called out.

"No one's here," Ryan said. He grinned, coming down the hallway. "Do you like my masterpiece?" He waved his hand up to the sky, gesturing to the bubble. "Did you know you could even do that? I guess I'm more powerful than you."

Laura shook her head. She was still in the process of learning about her powers before they were taken away from her.

"Where's Mom and Dad?" she asked.

"They went out," Ryan said. "Took their happiness from them too!" He laughed. "Oh, you should've seen them. They were so happy and in love. Disgusting! So, I decided to change it."

"Why are you doing this?" Laura demanded. She couldn't feel any anger though, although it was bubbling just below all the dark emotions. "Why steal my locket and make the world miserable?"

"I told you," Ryan said. "I want the whole world to feel what I feel. No one should be happy when I'm not, not even a little."

His eyes narrowed, and he looked right at Laura's heart. She looked down too, gasping. Little yellow light rays spluttered out, forcing their way forward.

Ryan saw them too. He reached forward and scooped some up, holding them in his hands. Ryan let the rays flop around for a bit, like water poured from a delicate vase.

"Where did you get this from?" he demanded.

"What do you mean?" Laura asked.

"You're happy! This is happiness!" Ryan narrowed his eyes, pushing the yellow rays into her locket that hung around his neck. "You were outside the bubble, weren't you?"

"I don't know what you're talking about."

"Where were you, Laura?" Ryan asked, his eyes growing darker and darker. "Who were you with? Answer me!"

"I didn't go anywhere," Laura stammered. "Leave me alone."

She pushed past him and stormed up to her bedroom, slamming the door shut behind her. Laura was done with this entire day. All she wanted was something to eat, and to sleep away the rest of the day. And to protect Lucas and her friends, of course.

She reached for her phone and sent a text to them all, asking how they were, hoping someone wasn't under Ryan's curse.

She didn't receive a single response.

From downstairs, she heard Ryan shout, "I'll find your last bit of happiness and destroy that too, just like I did to all your other emotions! You can't keep it from me forever."

Laura shot straight up, and she threw open her door. "Your bluffing!"

She slammed it shut again and locked it. Ryan mumbled something else, and Laura heard the front door close behind him. Her heart was beating fast again, and for once, Laura grew scared.

Ryan couldn't actually destroy *all* her emotions, could he? Unless he meant that he would use her locket to do so. Laura shook her head. No. It was impossible. But even worse, she grew more worried about Lucas.

She picked up her phone again and shot him a quick text, warning him about Ryan. Lucas wouldn't see the text until later, but she hoped Ryan had no idea what she was up to.

With her stepbrother out of the house, Laura finally decided to create a plan. She had no idea why Ryan was doing all this or where to even begin to stop him, but she was determined to find out in any way she could.

That kiss with Lucas reminded her of her strength, that not even the power of her locket or Ryan could steal away what was already inside her.

Laura rolled off her bed, unlocked her door, and went down the hallway. She tried to open Ryan's bedroom door, but of course, it was locked. Things couldn't be *that* easy, could they?

She sighed heavily and strolled to the bathroom, digging around in her drawer. She found a stray bobby pin at the bottom and grabbed it. Laura nodded and jumped up, making her way back to Ryan's bedroom. She stood next to the door, hoping it was the same exact lock as her own door.

Sticking the bobby pin into the lock, Laura wiggled it around for a few minutes, until finally, there was a quiet click.

"Yes!" she cried soundlessly.

Laura pushed open the door and stepped into her brother's room.

It was dark and a little dusty. His room was a mess and covered in trash. Laura pushed her way through, trying to not disturb anything. She looked around for a notebook, a laptop, or anything that could help her understand Ryan's plan more.

Finally, she found an old photograph turned upside down. There was Ryan as a kid, with another boy. They were both smiling happily at a park. She put it back and found a small notebook tucked under his bed.

Laura picked it up and flipped through the pages. She paused on one entry that stood out to her the most:

I don't need a new dad. I don't need a new sister. I don't care who they are; I just want my old family back. I just want my friend, Johnny, back. But if this new man makes my mom happy, I guess I can put up with them for a little longer. I think the girl is an empath. She's got so many colors just dripping off of her. I can see them. Maybe she can help me someday.

Laura frowned. She continued to flip through the notebook until she found a page just covered in black scribbles. Both pages were full, with nothing else but that. Curious, she flipped it to the next page and read the entry:

Johnny says he'll be okay. He's going to the hospital tomorrow. I made him promise I would see him tomorrow. And he did. See you tomorrow!

Laura gasped and quickly flipped open to the front of the notebook, reading from the beginning. She spent the next hour and a half pouring over her stepbrother's story. He wasn't much of a writer and used a lot of pictures rather than words. She read about when he met his best friend and how close they grew over the years.

Laura read about Johnny's illness, one that Ryan went on several hospital trips for so he could be with his friend. She turned the pages, learning more and more about who her stepbrother truly was. Ryan and Johnny were inseparable, adventuring together and doing literally everything together, and when he died, he left behind a hole in Ryan's heart that no one could fill.

When she got to the page full of black scribbles again, a tear slipped down her cheek. Everything made complete sense to her now. Now, she understood why Ryan was so angry and bitter all the time. Laura sighed and looked around, finding the box where the rest of the notebooks were hiding.

Inside the box were a dozen or so broken art supplies, along with a few more photos of Ryan and Johnny. She grabbed a photo near the top of the pile, tucked it into her pocket, and ran out of his room, but not before putting his notebook and box back to where they were when she found them. She left one of the photos of the two friends facing right side up and smiled.

Maybe that would help her brother remember what it felt like to love and be happy.

As Laura ran across the hallway and down the stairs, she pulled her phone out of her pocket and called Lucas.

"Hello?" he answered sleepily.

"I know how I can help my brother," she said. "Can we meet up tomorrow?"

"Sure, where?" Lucas asked.

"Anywhere."

"How about the coffee shop on 31st?" Lucas suggested. "3pm?"

Laura nodded. "Works for me!" She paused before hanging up and looked around. "Lucas, I love you, with all my heart. I promise I will fix all this. Just hang in there for a little bit longer."

"I love you too, Laura. I trust you." He hung up.

Laura smiled for a moment, but it fell away when she saw Ryan close the front door behind him.

He grinned, "So, that's where your happiness is coming from? Your boyfriend?" he mocked.

"What are you talking about?" Laura asked, pretending to be naïve.

Ryan grinned. "It's that one guy you always hang out with at school, isn't it?" He laughed. "Oh, man, this just makes things even better. Now, I know how to really *destroy* you."

Laura froze. She didn't realize Ryan even paid attention to her social life, then again, he would. She shook.

"What are you going to do?" she whispered.

"Same thing I did to everyone else!" Ryan laughed. "So, tomorrow then?"

Laura's phone fell out of her hand. "Don't you dare hurt him!" she shouted. "You can't do that!"

"Everyone's going to know my pain soon enough," Ryan said. "Everyone. I don't care who I have to hurt." He pushed Laura aside and started to climb the stairs.

"Why?" Laura asked him. "Why are you doing this?"

Ryan paused in the middle of the staircase. "I already told you."

Laura shook her head. "Not just that," she said. "Don't you know that there are people who can help you? That there are innocent people you're destroying just because you feel hurt?"

"I don't need help," Ryan said, turning away.

"You do," Laura responded. She looked at her stepbrother, the sadness she felt for him welling up inside her. "I've known that ever since we met. I didn't know it then, but I can see it now. You need to talk to someone about what you're feeling inside. It's not safe to hold in all your emotions like this." She paused. "You can talk to me. You just need to give me back my locket."

"So you can undo everything?" Ryan shouted, turning around. "Change how people feel? Not a chance!" He laughed and pulled Laura's locket out from around his neck. He waved it back and forth, grinning. "You won't need this anymore," he said. "It's too late to help me. It's too late to help anyone."

Ryan tucked it back under his shirt and continued up the stairs, disappearing down the dark hallway.

The front door opened again, and their parents came in, laughing about something. Laura turned to them, looking at her dad and stepmom. They didn't seem to be affected by Ryan's sadness bubble that was dangling over the city.

Yellow squiggles and shapes floated around them, pushing back the sadness and grief that tried to shove their way into their own little bubbles, almost like it tried to do to Lucas.

"Hi, Laura," Cassandra greeted when she saw her. "Did you have a good drive with your friend?"

"Good to see you home safe and sound," her dad added with a smile. "Looks like you need to get some rest. You look as pale as a ghost."

Laura nodded. "I know, I will," she lied.

She quickly ran up the stairs and quietly pulled out her notebook to organize her ideas, wondering how her parents were so unaffected by Ryan's powers. She thought about it for a little longer as she tried not to make too much sound, and wondered if there was a way to put a stop to Ryan's sadness, to make him love life again.

No matter what happened, she would help her stepbrother, even if it took all of her energy to do so.

***

The next morning, Laura woke up and found Ryan gone. She quickly dove for her phone and called Lucas to say good morning. When he responded, she let out a huge sigh.

"I thought he got to you already," she said in relief. "I was so scared."

"Is that the big bubble of sadness madness talking, or you talking?" Lucas asked.

"Both," Laura said. "I think the fear is just the worst right now."

"I'll be fine," Lucas said. "Don't worry about me. See you at 3, right?"

"Yes, I'll be there!" Laura confirmed. She sighed again. "See you soon."

She hung up and rolled out of bed. Slowly, she got ready for the day. It was the first day she decided not to wear sweats and a baggy t-shirt, or her hair up in a messy bun like she did for weeks when her mood was down.

Instead, she grabbed one of her cutest dresses, a pair of floral sandals, and braided her hair. Part of it was for Lucas, the other part was to make herself feel better and livelier. If she could escape the power of the bubble, so can everyone else.

Stretching, Laura looked at herself in the mirror. For the first time in a few weeks, Laura actually looked like herself. She took a deep breath and let it go.

"You got this," she whispered. "You can do this today. No backing out now."

For the rest of the morning, Laura wandered around her house, eating a bagel and drinking some orange juice. It was quiet. Cassandra had already left for work, and her dad was still sound asleep. It was a late night for them both, staying up late to finish up some things they had to do for work. Laura often forgot how difficult it must be to be an adult since being a teenager was hard enough already.

Laura finished her bagel and cleaned up around the house. Finally, she stretched, grabbed her house keys, bus pass, and her purse before heading out the door.

She still had a few hours to kill, so Laura decided to take a short walk around her neighborhood, hoping to get some fresh air before she headed over to see Lucas. She walked slowly at first, taking in all the views and smells of the streets.

She could smell the delicious aroma of freshly-baked bread coming from the bakeries and cafés, where people sat on the chairs outside and sipped their cups of coffee. Autumn was in the air, and soon, winter would be here. Laura wondered what the city would look like covered in a blanket of snow.

She walked to the end of her street, turned the corner, and checked the time. The coffee shop she needed to be at was only half an hour away, so Laura searched for the nearest bus stop. She climbed on the first bus and took her seat. The bus lurched forward and started to drive away.

Laura stared out the window, watching all the cars and buildings pass by. Everyone *did* look much sadder than they had been a few weeks earlier, and Laura crossed her fingers, swearing to help each and every single one of them regain their happiness as soon as she could get her powers back.

Finally, Laura arrived at the coffee shop. Lucas was already outside, sitting with two hot coffees and a couple biscotti. He waved to her, and Laura skipped off the bus. She hugged him, gave him a kiss on the lips, and sat down, taking the first sip of the coffee.

"I think I needed this," Laura said after a few minutes of silence.

"What? Coffee?" Lucas asked with a smile.

Laura thought he always had the most beautiful smile she had ever seen.

"No," Laura answered. "To get out and about in the city. Seeing all the miserable people up close, it makes me want to help even more."

"You will," Lucas assured her. "We just have to find out how to get that locket back."

Laura nodded. They sat there for a while, sharing the plate of biscotti and talking about how life in the city would be like if everyone were happy.

Laura told Lucas everything that she had discovered about Ryan, from his past to why he was acting out like he was. When she finished, Lucas reached out and held her hand. Before he could say anything, his eyes grew wide. Laura turned around and saw her stepbrother walking towards them.

"So, this is the boy," Ryan said with a grin as he pointed a finger at Lucas. "How are you not sad?"

Lucas shrugged. "Just lucky, I guess."

"Well, you won't be able to say that in about a few seconds, not after I'm done with you," Ryan snapped. He charged forward, but Laura stood in front of Lucas with her arms spread out, shielding him from Ryan. "And what do you think you're doing? You can't protect your boyfriend, especially not without that locket."

"I will *not* let you touch him. You'll have to go through me first!" Laura declared. "I know about Johnny!"

Ryan froze and stared at her. "How?" he whispered. "Did you go into my room?" Ryan charged at her instead, grabbing her wrists. He dug his elbows into her arms, pressing her to the ground. "How dare you invade my privacy? You leave Johnny out of this and *never* mention his name ever again! I will take every ounce of your emotions away, despite what I have to do."

"You can't," Laura whispered, feeling weaker and weaker.

When she couldn't move anymore, Ryan sprung up and charged towards Lucas, stealing away some of his yellow rays of happiness before running away. Lucas managed to get up after a struggle and walked over to Laura.

He smiled. "You're still happy?" Laura asked.

"He only took a little bit. I still have plenty left inside me," Lucas said. He helped her up. "You're not looking too good," he whispered. "Let's get you home."

Chapter Eight
Inside All Along

Laura stood in front of Lucas' car while still clutching tightly to his hand. She turned to Lucas and looked at him.

"He didn't affect you one bit. He couldn't," she whispered. "My parents weren't affected either."

"What do you mean?" Lucas asked.

"You have this golden dome surrounding you," Laura explained. She looked at Lucas again, watching his happiness bounce off of it for a moment before settling down with the dome. "And it just grows bigger and bigger."

"Have I always had this dome?" He asked, a quizzical look crossing his face.

Laura shook her head. "It only started after we got closer to the sadness bubble."

She let go of his hand, thinking. *How could that have happened?*

She didn't have her locket on her, and her powers were useless. But then again, she was feeling happy with Lucas. Laura paced back and forth, voicing out all her thoughts to Lucas, who nodded and listened intently.

When she finally paused to take a breath, Lucas grabbed her hands and pulled her close.

"Laura," he said, lifting her chin up. "Is it possible that your locket didn't have any powers after all?"

"That's impossible," Laura shouted, shaking her head. "It's always been in my family, passed down from generation to generation. They have all used it for their powers! That's how it works!"

"What if it's just part of it?" Lucas asked. He squeezed her hands. "What if most of your powers have been inside you all along?"

Laura let go of his hands and looked to the ground, thinking hard about what he had just said. She thought about the times when she didn't have the locket, remembering all the times she was able to help someone, locket or no locket. She blinked and blinked again.

Looking up at Lucas, she wiped away a tear. It wasn't just any tear, but a happy one. For the first time in months, the sparkle in Laura's eyes whenever she smiled came back. Not just the little ones she had now and again, but this time, she felt like her true self.

Her feelings flickered for a moment, and the sadness tried to take over her again. She stumbled forward, and Lucas caught her.

"I don't think I can do this," she whispered. "It's just too much."

Lucas frowned and steadied Laura. "Are you sure it's someone else's sadness you're feeling? And not your own?"

Laura shook her head. But deep down inside her, she knew. She gasped and looked up at Lucas, realizing all her mistakes. With all the sadness she felt from losing her mom, the lonely nights she and her dad spent alone years after that, and finally, all the big changes recently, Laura knew she had been holding them all back.

It only took Ryan's crazy havoc on the world to remind her that it was okay to be sad once in a while, that it was only healthy to feel all sorts of different emotions. Tears started to roll down her cheeks, and she held tightly onto Lucas.

"You're right," she whispered. "I've been holding all my sadness back for too long."

They sat down on the curb, and Laura cried. She let all her tears fall out and didn't feel bothered by her internal pain. The pain and the sadness were all there, but she took a deep breath and let the heaviest burdens in her mind flow out of her.

She saw her own sadness bubble turn slowly back to yellow, and finally, she took another deep breath. Laura looked up at Lucas.

"How am I supposed to face my stepbrother?" she asked. "I barely feel like I can do anything right now. I still feel too weak and too broken."

"You can do it," Lucas said. "I believe in you."

Believe... the word bounced around in her head. Laura nodded and clenched her fists. "I have to talk to Ryan. I have to talk to him and straighten this whole thing out," she said, standing up.

"That's what I'm going to do." She smiled again. "Thank you, Lucas."

"For what?"

"For helping me get back to normal," Laura answered with a laugh. "And now, I need to thank my stepbrother." She laughed again. "For showing me how to be sad."

Laura held out her hand and helped Lucas up. He grinned and dug into his pocket for his keys. They got into the car and drove out of the parking lot and down the street. Of course, traffic decided to pick up then and there, and they passed by a huge car accident on the way home. Lucas drove through the city, finding back roads to get to her house faster and faster.

Finally, they arrived at her house. Her dad was gone, probably went out to buy groceries or to run other errands. But Laura had a feeling that her brother was home. She could sense his presence. She jumped out of the car, burst through the door, and ran into the house.

Ryan was sitting on the couch, eating popcorn, and watching a movie. Laura slowed down, jumped over the couch, and landed next to Ryan.

"What do you want, weirdo? I'm not giving you your locket back," Ryan declared.

"Nothing much," Laura said. "I just wanted to say thank you." Laura reached her arms around him and gave him a long hug.

Ryan paused the movie before turning his head towards Laura. "For what?"

"For reminding me what it feels like to be sad," Laura replied.

Ryan froze. He turned slowly to look at her in confusion. Laura reached forward and hugged Ryan tightly again, sending a bit of happiness his way. A few tears rolled down his cheeks, and the remote fell out of his hand. He slowly reached up and hugged Laura back.

"I'm here if you ever need to talk," Laura said. "I'm sorry for going through your stuff. I just wanted to understand you just a bit better."

Ryan nodded. He shook in her arms and sat up, wiping his tears away. "I'm sorry," he whispered. "For everything."

"It's okay. I understand. Can you take the big bubble of sadness down now?" Laura asked with a smile.

He nodded again and closed his eyes. Lucas ran inside, with a big grin on his face upon seeing their reconnection. Laura gave

Lucas a smile that everything was going to be okay before turning back to her brother.

"Thank you, Ryan."

"Here," he said, handing her locket back. "I'm sorry for taking this. This belongs to you."

Laura smiled again and hung it around her neck. Right where it belonged. For the rest of the evening after Lucas had gone home for supper, Ryan and Laura watched movies together, just the two of them, bonding as siblings.

They talked about their powers, realizing how well they balanced each other out, and how similar they actually were to each other, more similar than they could've ever imagined.

"Maybe we can teach each other some things, train together," Ryan said.

"Yeah." Laura smiled as her yellow rays of happiness shined from ear to ear. "I'd like that a lot."

Locket of Emotions

LOCKET OF EMOTIONS

Locket of Emotions